"Why, you've got a picture of Dr. Manning," she said in surprise.

"You know her?" Her lodger sounded not too pleased.

"Used to work there. As a lady help, you know. But I didn't stick it. Couldn't do with her. Always following me about to see if I worked properly."

"She's very ill," said the man.

"*Is* she?"

"Very ill."

"D'you mean she's dying?" asked the landlady huskily; in a way she had liked Marion. Anyway, she wanted to think of her as in the land of the living. Alive to be grumbled about, not dead to be pitied.

"Yes," said the man slowly. "She will have to die. There's no hope for her."

———————— ★ ————————

Gwendoline Butler

DEATH LIVES NEXT DOOR

WORLDWIDE.

TORONTO • NEW YORK • LONDON
AMSTERDAM • PARIS • SYDNEY • HAMBURG
STOCKHOLM • ATHENS • TOKYO • MILAN
MADRID • WARSAW • BUDAPEST • AUCKLAND

To Aylmer Macartney

DEATH LIVES NEXT DOOR

A Worldwide Mystery/December 1994

First published by St. Martin's Press, Incorporated.

ISBN 0-373-26157-8

ONE

OXFORD, which presents so glamorous and beautiful a face to the world, has also its seedy side. The world of grey stone colleges and elegantly panelled common rooms is not the only one. Not all scholars are dons comfortably housed in college rooms with cheerful and dignified servants or live happily in North Oxford in a house with trees in front and a lawn behind. There is a sadder side made up of those who have not quite succeeded in the battle, a sort of sub-world of failures and hangers-on.

At the top of the scale are the newly graduated but not yet established, living outside college life but teaching for the colleges and looking at them with envious eyes. A fellowship is their ambition and they look at the possessors of them hopefully, longing for a death, an early retirement or a promotion. There are not nearly enough to go round. So for some hope dies, and some move away, while others obstinately linger on. If they linger long enough they sink towards the bottom of the scale where are all the people who should never have hung on at all, the people for whom Oxford represents a dream, a drug, an illusion. And these people you must pity because they are in thrall to a harsh deity who takes no notice of them and never will. Such people are the third class honours students, the women graduates who find an exciting world here they find nowhere else, the people who don't want to go home. They take poor teaching jobs, hack coaching, a job as a porter, as Father Christmas, a warder in Oxford prison by night, a poet and scholar by day, or so they hope, in order to hang on.

To this group are attached all the people who should never have been in Oxford anyway and would be banished if the Proctors knew they were there: the refugee who is so rootless that he has no real home anywhere except an attic in Wellington Square and who fills in his time and his pockets with a little odd blackmail, spying, and petty theft, and who is on the black lists of half the Embassies of Europe, even if low down: the actress without a play who hovers hopefully around the Playhouse and Ma Brown's café.

Prominent among this society is the perpetual scholar; the man who is always proceeding to the next and then the next degree. Labouring endlessly on theses which he may never present, eternally concerned with the minutiae of scholarship and losing the vitality, the perpetual scholar seems specially a product of the nineteen forties and fifties, of a society lavish with grants, eager to compensate for the security it cannot really provide.

Geographically this world centres on Wellington Square and Walton Street, although of course its members may be found anywhere. The hallmark of their lodgings is that they live in a contrived sort of way, with kettles hidden under the bookcase and dirty cups tucked neatly away in cupboards.

Because all the members of this world know each other or of each other, rumours spread rapidly; deliciously rapidly in the case of the rumour that the Dean of Gaveston was giving an open party which brought two-thirds of the members thirstily but mistakenly to the unhappy man's rooms. This day was afterwards known as the Glorious Thirst of June. Or with sinister rapidity as in the case of the present rumour, which was that in Oxford at the moment one was liable to be *followed*.

The gossip snowballed. Everyone adding his share.

Ezra added his.

Ezra found passing on the gossip a useful relief from thinking. Thirty-five years of being Ezra had accustomed him to all the thoughts he was likely to have, he didn't see much chance now of his thinking anything new, he was stuck with his old mind, with all its connections, associations and responses, and they were boring. He was even bored with his work. There was not the freshness to the study of Beowulf and Guthric that there had been ten years ago when he started it, he himself had not the same enthusiasm that he had felt when he had first landed in Oxford after five years in the army. That had been three years before starting on Beowulf so altogether he had been at it thirteen years now. Thirteen years too long possibly. It depended how you looked at it. You could say he was adding to scholarship, which was how Ezra's supervisor put it, or you could say he was wasting his time, which was how Ezra's father put it. Ezra himself put it half way between: he had added perhaps half a dozen new facts to the study of Beowulf, he had suggested a new interpretation of the Grendel figure (another myth, he thought) and he had enriched his own mind. If he had wasted any time it had been his own.

But so far it had not brought him any further in the world. He was still living in the same rooms in which he had set himself up ten years ago with an electric gramophone and an electric coffee pot as a student, he still had to hide his tea tray under the bed when his pupils came (he did a great deal of tutorial work for Prelims, grinding Anglo-Saxon into the heads of dull girls from St. Agatha's). In all this time it had never dawned on Ezra that his pupils could see his tea tray perfectly clearly under the bed drape. He always sat in the same chair. He had noticed however that the girls who had once seemed more or less his own contemporaries now got younger and younger every year and that he himself had almost got to thinking of them indulgently as pretty young things. He did occasionally ask them out for a drink or for dinner but now they always seemed shy and nervous whereas ten years ago everything would have gone bouncingly. He had no idea that his young pupils regarded his sombre good looks with respectful and romantic eyes: to them he was an elderly, but attractive figure, and it was a great treat to be sent as a pupil to him.

Out early one morning doing his marketing, which he did himself and on foot, for the sake of his liver (Ezra was something of a valetudinarian and took his health seriously), he met a young man with whom he had a party acquaintance.

"Hello, Ezra dear," said the young man. "Don't pad behind me so in your crepe soles."

"You nervous? Believe in this creeper?"

"Oh my, yes."

"Someone follows, you don't know it, and then suddenly there he is."

"Have you been followed?"

"Oh no, not me."

"Who then?"

"Not sure. I've just heard about it." The young man looked puzzled. Then his face cleared. "Everyone's talking about it. It must be true."

There were no details, but a sort of group conviction.

"This person *watches,*" said the young man.

Ezra raised his eyebrows and walked on thoughtfully.

At the delicatessen in the market the queue was standing peacefully reading and in one case apparently writing a book. Ezra took his place behind a large man whom he had certainly seen in the Bodleian working upon Bracton's 'De Legibus Antiquis'. Peeping, Ezra could see that his present study was the Newgate Calendar, which was roughly in keeping. But after a bit Ezra could see that he was really engaged in trying to make acquaintance with the tall girl in front, something of which he seemed to have small chance as she appeared at the moment to be interested only in Mrs. H's liver garlic sausage and the *Manchester Guardian*.

"Would you mind stepping off my foot?" she said sweetly, turning round. But after this Ezra saw to his amusement that they went away amicably together. You could never tell. Ezra nodded in approval. Over the years a grandfatherly attitude had grown up in him, a feeling that love and marriage were not for him. It had been unconscious, he had hardly noticed it, he thought, until lately, when it had taken a beating. It had been a peaceful state to be in, he recalled wryly.

As he thoughtfully pinched the lettuce for his dinner and eyed the rye bread to see if it was stale, the subject came up again. Mrs. Hofmanstall leaned over the sauerkraut and breathed her fears and garlic at him in the same breath.

"Of course it may not be true, Mr. Barton, I do not say it is, but my customers tell me." Mrs. Hofmanstall's customers told her everything; there was certainly every opportunity to as shopping there was a slow business. There was time for life friendships to be built up.

"Have you been followed?"

Mrs. Hofmanstall drew herself up. "Me? No. Naturalich not." She lowered her voice again. "All we hear is not right. It is not always follows. Sometimes he is there before."

Ezra said seriously: "You know there's a fallacy there somewhere, Mrs. H. But I get the feeling you describe. Nasty."

He gathered up his shopping and went on.

He continued his walk, through Market Street, down Cornmarket, under the trees of St. Giles, casting a longing but declining look at The Play-house beside whose doors he could see three of the people who amused him most and whom he most wished to impress. He squared his shoulders and assumed the stern look of a warrior king. One of the things Ezra did most was to act and they were casting for *Henry IV, Part Two.* He was longing to be the young Prince Hal. He realised however that he was most likely to get the part of the sick Henry IV. These were the parts he always got, he had been the King in *Hamlet* more often (he reckoned) than any man living. It was beginning to affect his character; you couldn't be called lecherous so often without beginning to feel it.

He cleared his throat and began to recite the great lines from Henry IV,

Oh sleep, O gentle sleep,
Nature's soft nurse, how have I frighted thee?

going through the catalogue of the sick king's symptoms and ending:

Uneasy lies the head that wears a crown.

Yes, he could see himself in the part. He could see Lamia Beauregard tossing her golden locks at the producer and he remembered how good, in a dreadful sort of way, she had been as Hamlet's mother. But then to be good in a dreadful sort of way was just what was demanded of Hamlet's mother. No doubt Lamia, an improbable but suitable name now he came to think of it, remembering Keats' girl who was metamorphosed into a snake, was not at all worried about anyone following her. Probably she expected that someone would be following her, just as she expected (and certainly would get what she expected) that she would soon go to London and throw her lustre upon such totally unknown stars as Dorothy Tutin.

He could see that Lamia was beckoning and after wondering whether it would look undignified or not to turn round and go, curiosity took him. After all he could walk down St. John Street to pay the call which he intended to pay before lunch and the thought of which was making a little warm fire of pleasure burn in his mind.

"We are talking about doing Ibsen," said Lamia at once.

"Well, I think I'm more of a Shakespeare man."

"There are other actors."

"Shakespeare's always safe," said the producer. "You can do him very badly indeed, and frankly we mostly do, and still get away with it."

"How are you getting on with *Henry IV, Part Two?*"

"Very nicely. We've got a lovely Harry," said the producer with enthusiasm, "just the right mixture of bounder and cad. No Henry IV yet though," and he looked thoughtfully at Ezra who sighed. Old dying Henry was just made for him.

"What about King Lear?" he suggested, remembering that there *were* great parts for dying old men.

"No part for me in it," said Lamia sternly. She knew her limitations, which included Cordelia.

"There are other actresses," he reminded her. "And other parts; what about Goneril and Regan?"

"Oh, that old bitch."

"I always think, Goneril and Regan, yes and Cordelia, too, are just the other faces of one personality," said the producer. "That's how I'd do it. All of them with the *same* face, only different. A triple split personality."

"And then you might have them all looking exactly like Lear," said Ezra entering into the spirit of the thing. "Which, when you come to think about it, is really most likely."

"I'm afraid it might seem a little like a Crazy Revue," said the producer regretfully. "Talking of Regan," he said, looking doubtfully at Ezra, "have you seen anything of Rachel lately?"

"Yes," said Ezra shortly. "And I don't know why she reminds you of Regan." The worst of being in love was that it made you so touchy.

"Oh, just the initials," said the producer. "I wanted to talk to her."

"She was at Marion Manning's. I'm on my way round to Marion's now." Marion's name produced the silence it usually did. She was a fabulous figure. But what did people really know about her? That she had been four years old when the First Great War started, in which her father had been killed, and only nine when it ended, and yet she had written one great poem on it which anyone would have been glad to have written, and then never touched the subject again. That she had become an anthropologist, been a member of a highly publicised and tragic expedition to Central America on which two men had died; that she had written a controversial book about it and then announced that anthropology did not provide the discipline she wanted, and turned herself into a philologist and a very good one at that, but that her name was still good for a paragraph in the Sunday newspapers. What did this young producer know about her? That he had seen her stocky grey-haired figure (with the slightly dragging left leg where the bomb had lamed her) at parties and heard her talking?

The three of them walked a little way with him before the producer looked at his watch and remembered a tutorial, and with an anxious look, which at once reduced his age by ten years (and, so Ezra thought, added them to his) disappeared.

"Give my love to Tommy," Ezra shouted. He knew the producer's tutor.

"Unless I have had some good things to say about the French Revolution I won't dare," called back the young man. The third member of the party was a silent young man from St. John's who had never in all the time Ezra had known him spoken one word, but drew constantly upon an old pipe and looked deep. Lamia and the silent man, who was continuing to look deep, went off together.

Ezra continued on his way down St. John Street and through Wellington Square to where Chancellor Hyde Street runs into Little Clarendon Street. When the houses it contained were built there were fields where Walton Street now lies. The houses were old pretty red brick cottages converted at great cost into cosy little houses watched over by the Georgian Trust. Marion lived in the corner house and although Ezra had got used to it the house was unmistakably Marion's.

Marion was standing in the window reading a book and her tom-cat, Sammy, was sunning himself in the garden. There was no love lost between Sammy and Ezra. Sammy raised his head as Ezra came past, and glared at him, slightly showing his teeth as he did so. All right, thought Ezra, if that's how you feel, I don't feel any better about you, and he bared his teeth back. The Professor of Morphology who was passing looked apprehensive, and Ezra realised sadly that the Professor, a nervous and humble man, had taken the threat as directed at himself. By the time he got to Marion's he was in a bad temper.

"I find the human race difficult and incomprehensible at the moment, Marion," he said, falling back into a chair.

Marion stood there running a hand through her short silver hair which seemed to shine with a light no one else's had; her bright friendly brown eyes looked at him with inquisitiveness.

"I don't suppose it's occurred to you to number yourself among the unaccountable?" Marion's tone was wry.

Ezra blinked.

"Oh, do you think so?" He considered. Perhaps this curious atmosphere he had noticed among his friends lately was coming from within him and not from without.

"I think I'm having an intellectual crisis!"

"What a luxury for you. I couldn't afford one." Marion was continuing in wryness. "Too old."

"You've had them though," pointed out Ezra, remembering the change-over from anthropology to linguistics. He looked at Marion and saw that she looked dry and thin. It struck him that he had not really observed Marion for a long time. She did look older.

"Oh, you have the special Oxford disease... Ennui, reluctance, it comes over everyone. Closely related, I always think, to the medieval 'accidie', one of the seven deadly sins, you may remember. Sloth is its other name."

Ezra flushed. Marion could always sting.

"It especially attacks intellectuals. I suppose you count as that?"

"You've brought me up to be one." Ezra regarded Marion as his intellectual mother. He hardly remembered his real one. Marion, however, was not obviously maternal. He had come to her for teaching in his first term, young and earnest, and she had moulded him. It was going to be difficult to tell Marion what he wanted to tell her.

"I begin to feel that perhaps I'd better get away and strike out in a new sea."

Marion frowned.

"I've had a sort of offer," he hurried on. "From Bridport. You know John Farmer has the new Chair, he's sort of offered..."

"Oh, *there!* They have a vested interest in mediocrity there."

"That's unfair." He wanted to say, "Hold back your blows, Marion," but he could see she was deeply hurt.

"Go if you like." She shrugged.

That was the trouble, Ezra did not know if he did like. He was happy here. He loved the rhythm of his life, the autumn and winter for quiet work, his acting in the spring and summer, the cheap trips abroad; in some moods he even loved his pupils. He knew all the little side streets of Oxford. Blue Boar Lane which lets on to the back premises of Christ Church and the houses, so like country mansions, of the Canons of the Cathedral. He knew and loved Magpie Lane and New College Lane and the tiny stretch of Catte Street. As a ghost, thought Ezra, this would be the world he would haunt, these loved little streets. He had walked them in the autumn when they smelt of wood smoke, and when they were frosty with snow, but he thought he liked them best in the summer. If condemned ever to be a revenant it would be to this summer world he would come back, walking the streets on warm moonlit evenings, dreaming of long-dead Commemoration Balls and evenings on the river. (In real life Ezra was a poor hand with a punt and hardly ever went near the water, but a ghost, of course, would be able to do everything.) Or perhaps the ghosts of the dancers and the musicians would be there, too, and he would hear music floating across the wall from Merton or over from the New Buildings at Magdalen which were new when Dr. Johnson was a young man. He loved all this and didn't really want to be uprooted, but Rachel, with her acid clear judgements, had changed everything. His indecision was mirrored in his face and Marion saw it.

"And who's been suggesting all this to you?"

"No one," said Ezra, deeply troubled; he was doing this so badly.

But Marion knew the answer to her own question. "Rachel, I suppose. John Farmer knows her father, of course."

She sat down at her desk and drew a thin brown hand across it for a cigarette. "Dusty," she observed. "I don't keep this house the way I should." On the top of her desk was a picture of a young man wearing an open-neck shirt and nursing Sammy.

Ezra walked over and picked up his photograph. "I was quite chubby then, wasn't I?"

Marion nodded.

"You were good to me then, Marion. I wonder why? I must have been a boring boy."

"Not so bad as some," said Marion philosophically. "And very attractive. I couldn't help noticing that." She smiled, and the bright brown eyes were set in a lace of little crinkles.

"I do depend on you, Marion."

"Not in all things," she said sharply.

"No. But to keep me on a straight level." Did Marion depend on him? And in a moment he knew she did.

It came to Ezra sharply then that Marion was one of the people he most loved in the world. Until six months ago he would have said *the* person.

And she had aged. Grown thinner, tenser, more strained.

"What's done this to you, Marion?" he heard himself say, to his embarrassment.

He saw great tears fill the brown eyes and it was like seeing the Pyramids weep.

"Marion!" he cried.

She mumbled something he could not hear. Then she repeated it.

"I'm being watched."

The words struck him unpleasantly.

"I saw a man killed once. I saw his eyes crossed in death. I felt he was watching me. Since then I've hated people watching me."

Ezra knew she referred to the death so many years ago of the man on the expedition. It came as a shock to him that Marion should refer in tones which so clearly showed that the wound was still there, raw and unhealed, to an incident he had thought long buried, far back in her past.

"No need to be so upset," he said, startled into unsympathy.

"You try it some time." Marion dried her eyes. "It's unnerving. I don't know this man from Adam. Or I didn't."

"Oh, it's a man?"

"Yes," said Marion shortly.

"Is he always there?"

"No." In spite of herself Marion laughed. "Only human. Not all the time."

"Are you sure? I mean, supposing he really is watching, are you sure it is you?"

"Quite, quite certain. He follows. Last week I went to London for the day. I saw his taxi follow mine to the station. Thursday I went to Stoke-on-Trent to give that lecture. He came, too. Don't say I should tell the police."

"No, I wasn't going to."

"There's been no threat, you see, no nuisance. He never tries to talk to me. Never comes even very close. But he's always there. Why?" She said slowly, "And yet I don't feel any malice in him. He's just *interested*. In me."

"Well, so are a lot of people, Marion." Ezra was thinking hard. So this was the basis behind all the rumours. Somehow it had got out. "Who have you told, Marion?"

There was silence.

"I have told no one. I swear. I have told no one at all."

But this rumour was all over town. Marion must have let it out. Or perhaps the neighbours had noticed.

"What about the neighbors?" he asked. "Do you think they've noticed? Or have you told them?"

Marion looked surprised. "I don't know them."

Ezra was half irritated, half amused. "You must know them, Marion."

"Why? I've never even seen them."

"Oh, you must have seen them. In the garden, digging or something."

"Oh, but I never go in the garden," said Marion, looking placidly at the jungle beneath her window. "Can't stand it. No, I tell you the neighbours are out. I haven't told them, and I don't believe they've noticed."

"People do know, though."

Marion had walked to the window. "Look out there."

Ezra pulled back the curtains and looked across the road to the junction of Chancellor Hyde Street and Little Clarendon Street. The wind that nipped that corner was usually chill and he was not surprised to see the figure standing there put its collar up. It was a small dark man with spectacles; he was wearing a mackintosh and underneath it a neat blue suit.

"He doesn't look like a detective," murmured Ezra.

"I'm sure he's not that." Marion spoke with decision.

Ezra looked round her quiet, green book-lined room. It was so difficult to associate Marion with all this.

"You stay here," he said. "I'm going out to have a closer look at him."

He shut Marion's front door behind him, shutting in a stray creeper or two as he did so. As he pushed his way through the massed vegetation to the gate, it occurred to him that while Marion might not know her neighbours, the neighbours almost certainly knew Marion and her weeds.

In the street, a lorry was drawn up discharging a load of coal and Ezra was able to come round the back of it and get close to the man before he had a chance to observe him.

The man was standing there, his feet planted a little apart, and his hands in his pockets. He was making no pretence of having a purpose in being there, and yet he was very unobtrusive, he slipped neatly into the background. There was something vaguely familiar about him, some quality that Ezra thought he knew. But it remained elusive. As Ezra watched, the man shifted his feet, scratched his hair, and settled his hat more comfortably on his head. Clearly he meant to stay where he was.

"I suppose he is watching Marion?" wondered Ezra.

At that moment a window slammed in Marion's house and the man swung his head round promptly to see.

Ezra stepped out from behind the coal lorry, and walked down Chancellor Hyde Street. The man watched him indifferently, although he must have observed him come from Marion's house and had probably been watching him. Ezra saw that the hands now rolling a cigarette were neat and not swollen by manual labour, there was a gold ring on the left hand; they trembled slightly.

At the corner Ezra turned and looked back. The road was quiet and empty except for the lorry and the watcher. A little ginger kitten ran across the road, it was calling out in shrill kitten's shrieks. It halted unsteadily in the gutter. The man called it to him, and stood for a few minutes with it in his hand, looking at it and stroking it. Ezra watching from a distance could have sworn there was liking, even affection, in the movements of those hands.

Till the kitten screamed. Ezra could not help thinking of Marion's narrow bones beneath those hands.

IT WAS TRUE, although Marion would not admit it, that she had from the first been much more aware of the man than had been apparent. She had noticed him before anyone else. She had such a quiet constricted life that a new face stood out at once. Besides, there was another reason.

It was not the first time: he was only one in a succession of such people. In her life she had had an inconvenient trick of picking up hangers-on in a way she could not quite account for.

There had been the man in Monte Carlo. An unlikely place for Marion the austere to be, but she had been on a visit to an old sick aunt. In the intervals between listening to Auntie's reminiscences of the Prince of Wales (she meant Edward VII, of course) and administering her medicine, she had escaped for long walks by the sea. The sea in spring there could be lovely and this had been in 1939 when people's nerves were on edge and perhaps inclined them to do odd things, but she did not think this *quite* explained the man. She had noticed him looking at her in the rose garden by the Casino: he had been looking at her expectantly as if he waited for her to speak. The oddest thing about him was that he knew where she lived; he was back there before she was, loitering again, expectantly. Expectant of what? Marion asked herself. Nothing that she was prepared to give anyway: he was a more rakish, selfish-looking man than Marion would have ever trusted herself to.

And there had been others, faces in queues that had grinned and nodded at her; hands waved from doors that *she* had never opened; feet that seemed to expect hers to fall in step with them.

Probably it was her appearance: Marion considered that she had a very usual, humdrum appearance; she was simply mistaken for someone else.

Even Ezra had his place in this queue. She recalled the young earnest Ezra wearing his scholar's gown over a duffle-coat so that he looked as square as Tweedledee. He had waited outside the lecture-room to speak to her after her justly celebrated, and often repeated, lecture on "The Myth of Guthrum".

Then she laughed.

Perhaps it was unfair to number Ezra among them: admittedly he had seemed to know exactly what he wanted from her. A reference to a book she had mentioned in her lecture; was she certain she had got it right? Marion was certain; faced with such unusual assurance she was at first angry, then amused, and finally friendly. Afterwards she had understood that it was the assurance of utter ignorance; once Ezra had learnt the way around his world he would never have dared approach a lecturer with such a comment. By nature he had too little assurance, not too much.

Marion shook her head; no, Ezra was something else again, and not one of the strange people who seemed to pop up in her life. After all he was still in her life, and the marked thing about the others was that after a time they disappeared. They lost heart, gave it up, and went.

Or they had done so far. Unhappily this man seemed more persistent. She tried to laugh it off, to see it in its proper proportions. She told herself that some people had allergies, others had second sight, or what their best friends wouldn't tell them, or some other social drawback; she had this.

Only it had not happened for some time, indeed had never before happened in Oxford.

Perhaps this was why for the first time she was taking it seriously instead of half dismissing it, as she had always done up to now, as imagination or coincidence.

And also this man seemed so quiet but determined. She really couldn't doubt that he was watching her, Marion.

She was aware of him throughout the quiet routine of her day. She usually got up early in the morning, went down, got in the papers and milk, then returned to bed with coffee and toast. She slept lightly and badly and was always glad to begin the day again. Marion was an optimist; however tire-

some yesterday had been, and however unpromis-
ing today looked, she always started off the day
with a little glow of happiness. The man was never
at his post in Chancellor Hyde Street as early as
this, but by about eleven in the morning he had arrived unobtrusively and was watching her. Some
days if she went off on a journey he followed, on
other days she was able to leave him behind. He
had, for instance, twice come after her to London
and once when she went to the Midlands to give a
lecture. It had occurred to her once or twice that it
was a question of money whether the man trav-
elled with her or not: when he had enough, he
came; when he had not, he stayed behind. What she
could not arrive at was his motive. She thought he
was trying to observe all he could about her; he
wanted to know exactly what she was like. "He
seems to want to know if I am *me*," thought Marion indignantly.

She for her part was watching him, but she never
could get very close. She had once, on Oxford station, taken her courage in both hands and marched
up to him.

"Well," she said fiercely. "Do you know me?"
She had been close enough to him then to see the
slight jaundiced yellow under his pallor and to see

the fine little lines round his eyes and mouth. He was younger than she was but still not young.

He had said nothing, nothing at all.

"Someone should teach you not to stare," she had snapped, and she had felt herself grow red and cross.

It was at this moment she swore she saw recognition in his eyes.

Later she had looked at herself in her bedroom mirror and shaken her head. "Poor battered tired old Marion. Do you imagine you are still a femme fatale?"

It had been one of her old bitter jokes to call herself a fatal woman. She had been fatal enough for poor Francis, in her fashion.

From then on she had dismissed any thought of going to the police. She could imagine only too well how she would be received: the raised eyebrows, the sceptical smiles; the advice to see a doctor.

She was under the care of a doctor in any case. Dear Dr. Steiner had been fumbling about, trying to find a cause and hence a cure for her headaches, for about a year now. "I can give you aspirins, Marion," he had said. "I can alleviate the pains but we must find out what is *causing* them." Marion had answered that she would be quite glad just to have alleviation. "It's hindering my work, you know." Dr. Steiner had looked at her for a long time before answering. "Ah yes, your work. You think a good deal about that?"

Marion had nodded. It had been a rather one-sided conversation, as it was more or less bound to be, considering the doctor was peering down her throat with a light. "And do you dream a great deal, Marion?" This time Marion had shaken her head in a no. But it was not true; she did dream; she dreamt a great deal.

She thought she could blame herself for this. There was another side to Marion of which her colleagues knew nothing, of which Ezra knew nothing, and of which the doctor knew nothing; she had another world, and it was this world which had triggered off her dreams.

Every week she visited the children's wards in the tall, old hospital near where she lived; she played with them, talked to them and tried to distract them. Boredom is a great hindrance to recovery. In this world she was a different person, she was slow moving, almost phlegmatic, calm. She was better tempered, too. So there was the academic Marion, the home Marion, the poetic Marion, and the hospital Marion. She had no name there; she was known as the Play Lady. Presumably someone, somewhere, in that great building knew her as Dr. Manning, but the name was lost.

She valued this world of hers; she had found the entrance to it herself. She had gone to visit a friend and had wandered by mistake into the wrong ward. Her entrance was welcomed, and since Marion was at heart an entertainer, she could not help but respond. She amused them. She promised to return next week and she did so, and the week after. Very soon she was an accepted institution. She took them books, odd toys, and games, and wandered round from child to child. This period was the best time of all and would probably have gone on if some child had not discovered that Marion's stories and talk were better than any book.

She was missed when she was away. The children were accusing, with the unashamed egotism of those who know beyond a shadow of doubt that they are the centre of all possible worlds. "Why were you away last week? We missed you."

"Like me to read?" asked Marion, always equable with them. "Or play card games? Or sing to you?"— She did sing sometimes in a low, tuneful, untrained voice.

"Talk."

"That's the hardest work of all." But she sat down with a smile. The children asked her 'just to

talk' more often than anything else. She told them
the most wonderful things and although they did
not always believe them they drank in every word.
She told them of things that had happened to her
and stories she had heard. They were real life stories, and although the children were sceptical in fact
she invented nothing; she would have preferred to
read or play dominoes but very well, if they wanted
her to talk, then she would talk.

As the weeks went on Marion's talks got more
and more vivid but she did not notice. The children noticed, however, and their excitement was
reflected in their quickened pulses, raised temper-
atures and restless nights.

It took some time for the nursing staff to relate
all this to Marion's visits, but they did so in the end.
Even then they could not at first guess why such a
quiet person could have such a stimulating effect.
A nurse lingered one afternoon to listen and observe.

"It's all quite harmless," she reported afterwards. "That is, she only tells them stories from her
travels in South America and so on, and it is absolutely fascinating, and educational as well. I don't
wonder they love it. But still," and she shook her
head, "it's the *way* she tells it: as if she were there,

she's reliving that past of hers. And I don't think she even knows she's doing it.''

So a gentle hint was passed on to her and Marion woke up to what she was doing. All story-telling from her own experiences was stopped and she stuck wryly to Cinderella. But inside her the stories went on. The past which she had comfortably laid away all those years ago was still alive and kicking.

It shook her up and reminded her that life was not a Pandora's box which you could put the lid on and forget. Her headaches started again and drove her to seek the doctor's advice. She thought his remark about dreams acute, but she was inclined to resent it. He could confine himself to her pains and leave her to cope with her dreams. So she shook her head.

Quite often she dreamt of the past but sometimes she dreamt of the future. She dreamt that the book she was working on was completed but that it had been burnt before she could get it to the publisher's hands. She had dreamt this dream in varying forms more than once. Surely fire in dreams meant something rather nasty in Freudian terminology? It seemed a pity that it had to be associated with her poor little book. Characteristically Marion took her studies lightly. She knew her own value as a scholar and did not overrate it. She was a subordinate, a contributor, not an originator, not a hacker-away in new and virgin territory. She had had much praise, but it was beyond her deserts.

Marion had a keen idea that some of her colleagues were cautious, if not suspicious, of her. Sitting in the Common Room, or working in the Library, she felt their quick glances and their little silences. She was an outsider, never quite one of 'them'; a changeling who had had too much publicity; more than was good for her perhaps.

A good deal of this feeling was caused by her changeover from one school of studies to another. She was only a tolerable English scholar but potentially she had been much more as an anthropologist. She knew this and everyone else knew it. So her transference puzzled them.

On this subject she had kept her own counsel. She never spoke of it. No one thought this odd of her. It was merciful that she lived among women who distrusted confidences and too much talk about self. They thought *she* was odd but not her silence.

What would they have said, she wondered, if they knew the real cause for her silence? She was silent because there was practically nothing she could say. She could never speak professionally again about her old subject; she had forgotten everything she knew. When she came round to life again after her husband's death she had found that all her knowledge, all her carefully acquired techniques had been erased from her mind. Six years of work had gone in a few hours. She was not only ignorant, she was worse than ignorant, her mind blocked all further studies on this subject. Marion knew when to take a hint from the Gods; she rebuilt her life on different foundations.

But it was not a story she wanted her sober, realistic, feet-on-the-ground companions to know.

Down in the kitchen below Marion's sitting-room Joyo was also watching the man from the window. She was as aware of his presence as Marion, but in a different kind of way. But Joyo was a different sort of person. She was small and sturdy and given to wearing bright peasant clothes. Joyo was not her real name, of course, but one she had adopted in defence against her real one, about which she preferred not to think; she had got it as a matter of fact from a gay Australian in the canteen where she had worked during the war. The war had been Joyo's apogee, frankly she had never had it so good again. The laughter, and the crowding together, and the tension, even the danger, had suited her. She had

been out, free. And then, the war over, back she
was obliged to pop like Cinderella. She had a gay
volatile temperament, although in her bad moods
or when her head ached it was as well to keep out
of her way.

But it was a bright cheerful face which stared
from the window now. She was passionately interested in the Watcher, and unlike Marion would
have liked to have asked him into the house. But
being more worldly than Marion she could also see
the danger.

She moved across the kitchen idly picking up a
bit of pastry off the cinnamon apple tart as she
passed, and then suddenly doing a little dance in the
middle of the kitchen, just because the floor was
bare and sunny. She looked at her face in the mirror. The bright orange lipstick which had so capti-
vated her in the advertisements shone on her lips.
Joyo kept a supply of makeup in the kitchen cup-
board in a box labelled Oxo. It made her feel gay
when the world was dull. It was a little secret she
kept from Marion, although privately she thought
Marion must be pretty slow not to have discovered
it. She poked at her treasures, lipsticks, nail var-
nish, powder and scent. There was also a photograph in there which she studied with interest. It
was not of anyone she was fond of, or indeed of

anyone she had ever known, but it had won a
money prize for her and Joyo, who was a frugal
soul, appreciated that. She tucked the money into
her purse. She dabbed a little scent behind her ears
before going to look in the oven. She would have
liked to have her hair dyed that deep mauve she so
much admired, but she feared that it might embar-
rass Marion, not that Marion and Joyo always saw
eye to eye by any means, but they had lived together for so long now that Joyo had learnt how far
she could go.

Joyo looked wistfully at the coalman delivering
coal next door but one. She fancied she knew his
face. He turned, and she was quite sure: she had
seen him at the little café down by the station where
they played music and where she enjoyed herself so
much when she got the chance. She had been there
last Wednesday and unless she was much mistaken
so had the coalman. He looked cleaner, of course
(not so much cleaner as the honesty which lay close
to the surface in Joyo obliged her to say), and he
looked happier. Indeed he had been very happy
dancing the cha-cha to a tune which had set Joyo's
feet tapping. She regretted that she had not been
dancing herself but her companion at the time, a
morose man from Manchester that she had met on
the railway station, had not, as he himself put it,

been much of a dancer. Joyo would never see him again and she did not care. She liked men and their company but she tried, as far as possible, to avoid permanent relationships. She would not, in any case, have wanted to know the Mancunian any longer. He had been tactless.

"You don't want to dance that sort of thing, my dear," he had said, patting her hand, "not at our age."

One offence: for Joyo did not care to be touched unless she said. Double offence: he was at least ten years older than Joyo. So she moved her hand hastily away and upset a cup of coffee over him. It was one of those things that Joyo could never be quite sure she had done on purpose or not. The coffee did him no harm so far as Joyo could see, but it had an immediate and savage effect upon his emotions. From a nice, polite, quiet if boring man who was just buying Joyo a friendly cup of coffee while he waited for his train, he was transformed into a loud talker and hard knee-gripper. Poor Joyo was horrified and at once began to think of ways to keep his voice and his hand down; she was experienced and wordly enough to recognise that it was for her to cope. Sadly she recalled the man in Bow who had climbed up the window curtains and the man in Southend who had crawled under the table. Neurotics seemed to be her lot.

Fortunately the stain of coffee on the cloth, long and boot-shaped, reminded him of Italy, and Italy of the Battle of Cassino.

"Here was us," he said, sprinkling sugar in a circle lavishly round the table. "Here were the Jerries," and a large amount of salt went down. "Here's the mountain," and he staggered over with the coffee urn, then to Joyo's horror began to look around for the Benedictine Monastery. There was a bottle of Benedictine on a shelf within his reach and his hand stretched out for it. "Here we are," he said cheerfully, "very suitable." And the bottle went on top of the coffee urn. Joyo was heartily glad that the proprietor was on the telephone, and got to her feet with a view to slipping out.

Unluckily the coalman, who had finished his dancing, had also been at the Battle of Cassino.

"Here," he said. "Here, chum, you've got it all wrong. *We* were *here.*" He sugared yet another area of the cloth. "And the Jerries were *here.*" This time he used pepper and Joyo at once began to sneeze loudly.

"Naw," said a third man also coming over. "That's not right. What you want . . ."

"Were you there?"

"Naw," said the man, "never left England, not me. In a reserved occupation. But I've been watching Monty on television, see. He ought to know. You've got the monastery in the wrong place. . . . It was lower down."

Joyo was desperately embarrassed, and tried to look as though she had nothing to do with them, but they would not let her get away with this, and pressed her into service to stand between them as the Tenth German Army Group. A dangerous thing to be she began to feel as it looked as though the believer in the Up Monastery and the believer in the Down Monastery might come to blows over this issue before they could fight out the battle proper.

"You don't know nothing about it," sneered the coalman, rapidly seizing the bottle of Benedictine. "Everyone knows the ruddy old monastery was at the top. That's what the battle was about." As he spoke his fingers were quickly but almost absently undoing the bottle. He sniffed. "Only a dummy," he said, disappointed.

Joyo was under the table by this time, hoping that no one would notice her, but as she was still sneezing she was afraid they might. But the disappointment over the bottle, in which all three seemed to share, reconciled them and they sat down and began to talk over the Italian campaign. No one took any more notice of Joyo and after a bit she crept out from under the table and went home. But she saw the proprietor emerge fiercely as she left. It might be as well, reflected Joyo, to keep out of the Mocha Mecca for some time. Besides, she had a small memento of the Mecca in her pocket.

The coalman finished his job and the van moved off. It was easier now for Joyo to see across the road.

Yes, the watcher was still there. What was he doing? What was he doing in Marion's life? She felt sure he had come to see Marion. She felt a little premonitory thrill of terror.

And from her kitchen window she could see, what Ezra could not see, that Rachel was lurking in the corner between the house and high wall.

TWO

SOMEONE HAD ONCE CALLED Rachel the girl who knows everybody and there was a lot of truth in this. Rachel was of academic stock: a member of a real old Oxford family, as yet another friend had said. In fact, you might have said of three important Oxford families, all of them inter-married into one famous clan. The families were: the Leavers, the Boxers and the Hansoms; all equally distinguished and equally clever. Old President Leaver had had the honour, way back in the nineteenth century, of leading his college forward into the world of science; he was not a scientist himself, but he had seen the advisability of electing an eminent scientist to a fellowship at a time when this was not so common in Oxford. He had thus established himself for ever as an advanced man and his family were bound to be advanced and liberal also. It had sometimes been difficult for his descendants to be advanced and liberal enough, they had sought for causes to show their progressive minds, they had advocated votes for women and birth control, they had fought in the Spanish Civil War, and since then they had signed peace pledges, denounced colour bars and marched upon rocket bases. It was difficult for their fellow-citizens to deny that they were very often right in what they proclaimed, but all the same they were irritating people.

The Boxers had brought plain dottiness into the clan; it was a highly intellectual dottiness and, therefore, much prized in Oxford circles. Dr. Boxer was famous as the man who failed to remember the face of his own wife after an exceptionally dull dinner party at his own house and thrust her out into the cold after the departing guests with the remark: "Go home, dear lady!" He did not drink, so it was not to be explained that way. He was also noted for his command of seven different languages and for the polite abuse he could utter in all of them. He had been heard to boast in his high sweet voice when in the seclusion of his college common-room when his colleagues were occupied with port and thick cigars that he knew the verb "to..." (and here he would leave a blank and wag his wicked old white head and titter) in all European languages. His friends believed him and were impressed.

The Hansoms were something different again: they were the heavy-weights, the men you could be sure of. They went into the Foreign Service and had important embassies abroad, they were in the Treasury or the Cabinet Office, and just lately they had taken an interest in Television. But the Hansoms, scattered by their duties as they necessarily were, remembered that above everything they were an Oxford family. If any issue of importance came before Convocation, that vast gathering together of all Oxford Masters of Arts by which Oxford in theory alone rules itself, then you could be sure that the Hansoms would come cycling in from their country livings, or drive down in fast cars from London, or even fly in to prevent some disaster such as women taking degrees or W. H. Auden becoming Professor of Poetry; they were usually unsuccessful.

This ancestry had given Rachel great assurance, not social assurance, she hardly recognised the need for that, but intellectual assurance. With four generations of right thinking behind her, she felt convinced beyond the need even to consider it that the standards, values and judgements of her group and people like her were forever right.

Physically she took after her grandfather Boxer who had been a very beautiful man. In addition she had a sense of humour which may have come from him, too.

The combination of all these qualities, Boxer, Leaver and Hansom, was pretty paralysing and there were many who found Rachel a paralysing problem.

"I'd as soon make love to a man-eating spider," declared the young man who had complained that Rachel knew everyone.

Rachel had become an anthropologist and this was how she came Marion's way. She had read and admired the young Marion's study of the Alpha tribes of Central America and had sought her out. No one knew how Marion felt about being remembered as an anthropologist, Rachel was the first person who had had the courage to speak about it to her face. However, even Rachel found that Marion had her reserves; and yet a ·steely friendship grew up between the two.

In this friendship Joyo by no means shared, although there was a lot about Rachel that she ruefully admired. Together with a lot she didn't. She was sharp enough, however, to see that this cut both ways and that equally there was a lot Rachel would not like in her. She was careful as a result, so that while she knew Rachel it would be true to say that Rachel did not know her.

She watched the girl now, and wondered what she was about, standing there in the street. She looked cold, too, poor child. Joyo would have liked to call Rachel into the warm kitchen, but caution restrained her. Let Marion, kind old Marion, do that. Let her be the one to stick her neck out.

Ezra was thinking of Rachel as he stood on the corner of Chancellor Hyde Street. Behind his thoughts about Marion ran the steady stream of his preoccupation with Rachel.

He was horrified to see her suddenly walk forward from the corner and go straight to the watcher.

"What did you say to him?" he asked.

"I asked him the time," she looked up. "Go on, ask me why I asked him that?"

"Well, why?"

"I wanted to hear his voice."

Ezra raised his eyebrows.

"I'm pretty fond of Marion. The fact that I don't think she's good for you is another matter. She's not the only one who noticed him. I went to Stoke with her, you know. I saw him before Marion did."

"So—what about his voice?"

Rachel was impatient. "I wanted to hear what sort of a person he was. Not the sort of person to be remotely connected with Marion at all."

Ezra nodded. "But you make Marion sound a snob. She's known a pretty wide range of people in her day. She knew..."

"Yes, but they were clever people, or interesting people, or out-of-the-way people. This man is ordinary."

Ordinary, thought Ezra, remembering the kitten. Is he so ordinary?

"You're pretty much of a prig yourself, Rachel," was all he said mildly. He looked up at Marion's window and saw that she had gone back to work at her table by the window. He could see her intent profile, as she bent over a book. No good going back there now. Marion was miles away.

He turned his attention to his love.

"Why do you have to go round looking like the retreat from Moscow?" he asked her irritably. "You'd be quite a good-looking girl if you didn't get yourself up like that."

"It's so *cold*." The huge aquamarine eyes stared at him over the edge of a scarf. "Freezing. I've just come back from the Sudan, don't forget."

"Yes, I always forget you're the little anthropologist."

"Not a very good one." Rachel sighed. "Trouble with me is," she said wryly, "that I like the people I go to live and work among. And I want them to like me. Won't do. To be a good anthropologist you've got to be quite detached. I minded that those last people, the Berboa, didn't like me."

"Seems a reasonably human sort of thing to mind," said Ezra.

"It does, doesn't it? But that's it. Anthropologists are not human. Or only remotely, men-in-a-machine human."

"You must have picked up that style of dress from the Berboa," said Ezra, observing her affectionately.

Rachel ignored this. "Anyway who cares? To hell with intellectuals." This was the Hansom strain coming out—hotted up by the Boxer.

"Do you think I'm an intellectual?"

"Oh, so so," said Rachel absently from the security of her own intellectual eminence.

"You're honest, anyway," exclaimed Ezra, more than a little hurt.

"Let's look at it this way," said Rachel, coming back to earth with a start. "You're more of an intellectual than *me,* for I sometimes think that I simply inherit my way of life and that left on my own..."

"I think so, too," interrupted Ezra with satisfaction. So Rachel did sometimes see herself.

"But you're *less* of an intellectual than my Uncle Bertie," went on Rachel. Uncle Bertie was a professional philosopher, and although many philosophers are very practical men and keep a remarkably sharp eye on the world and its benefits, Uncle Bertie Boxer did not. He was so constantly engaged in his battle with words that to the lay observer he sometimes seemed not quite in his right mind. It *is* alarming to come across a middle-aged gentleman running through the University Parks muttering: Are questions constitutionally nosey?

"Thank God for that," said Ezra.

He wondered what Rachel got from him. Nothing more, probably, than an irresistible impulse to tidy him up. She wasn't at this stage in the least in love with him. He felt a desire to show off.

"In six years I shall be a Doctor of Philosophy, the acknowledged master of my little corner of research, cock of my own dunghill."

"In six years you will be forty-odd. You may be dead."

"You may be right," he admitted dolefully. But he had to go on.

"I have an idea about the figure behind a small group of Early English epic fragments. I think you can pick out some individual points about the writer. A sort of little Homer, well perhaps I exaggerate there, but still he was a *real* person. Anyway I want to reconstruct this lost man."

"A sort of Anglo-Saxon quest for Corvo?"

"Oh, that wonderful book!" Ezra was just the sort of person to be caught up in the spell of Corvo: he *liked* lost souls. "But I can never make up my mind whether it is fact or fiction."

"Never much interested in Corvo, I must say. He must have been a dreary little chap."

"I told you you were a prig. But, of course, what makes it so fascinating is what it reveals of the author."

While they were talking they had both been watching the man who stood there, oblivious to everything except the one house. His very concentration made Ezra feel uneasy.

"Could he be a detective?"

"Why should a detective watch Marion?"

"That's something we shall have to ask Marion," said Ezra, a trifle grimly.

"He's not a detective," said Rachel. "I'll swear to that. I've spoken to him and you haven't. He's not sharp enough." She had convinced herself anyway. "Besides, Marion's *good*. There can't be anything in her life that needs detecting."

Ezra was thinking.

He was remembering what he knew about Marion, what he had heard and what she had told him. With the interest in anthropology had gone a wide interest in people, everything had been grist to her mill. She had no more been able to avoid gathering up the curious, the strange and the lost people than now she could help gathering up the lame dogs she had known.

"Has it struck you that Marion must have known some pretty wicked sort of people in her time? Crowley and Beasley and Rosa Farmer and so on. Not a little bunch of honeys really."

Rachel frowned. "Silly rather than wicked," she said loftily.

Ezra sighed. "That's exactly you all over. Silliness doesn't rule out wickedness. Rather the reverse. Someone silly and wicked could be very dangerous."

"Do you think this man is dangerous?" Rachel was surprised.

Ezra nodded. He was convinced there was danger for Marion, and what was more he felt sure Marion knew it, too, in her heart.

They threaded their way through the crowds of undergraduates on bicycles and approached the School of Anthropology, which was housed in a large sunny building.

"I have to leave a note," explained Rachel, although she had no need to offer any explanations to her companion, who would have trotted along happily beside her to the moon if she had happened to suggest it. "And I've a book to pick up in the library. Do wait for me."

Ezra tucked his feet under a chair and sat down to wait. He was thoroughly happy in this atmosphere of leisurely learning. He realised anew how unsuited he was to leave it.

A few students drifted in and out, exchanging a word with the porter in his little cubby-hole as they did so. He was a round fat agreeable man and an old friend of Ezra's, who had waited here many times for Rachel. He came out now to talk to Ezra.

The porter and his wife knew both Marion and Ezra well.

("I suppose she feels sort of maternal to him," the wife had suggested.

"Oh no," said the porter.

"Not . . . anything else?" queried his wife doubtfully. She didn't want to think badly of Marion.

"Oh no, mother, you've got it all wrong. People like them have interests in common. That's how they put it. Things in common. Age doesn't count. It's their minds."

"Well I can't help thinking it's all a bit—" She hesitated: "Comic.")

"I'd be glad to have a word with you, sir."

"Do," said Ezra, looking up in surprise.

"I live in Little Clarendon Street, sir, as you know, just around the way from Chancellor Hyde Street, I'm often up and down the road, I usually go that way to the Parks to exercise my little dog. You've seen us perhaps, sir?"

Briefly Ezra let his mind rest on the dog; the 'little dog' was a great loutish retriever with teeth like a tiger's fangs and a temper notorious among even the ill-tempered dogs of North Oxford.

"Yes, I know him."

"And you being a particular friend of Dr. Manning's, sir, I thought I'd mention it."

"Mention what?" There was something coming.

"She's a decent sort. She was very kind to me and the wife when we lost the kiddie."

Ezra remembered that the porter's little daughter had died of a rare form of diphtheria.

"And we're not the only ones, she's always had a helping hand for people like us. And I mean a real helping hand. Have you ever noticed Dr. Manning's hands, sir? They're hands that work. Oh, I know you work, sir, what I mean is that Dr. Mar-

ion works with her hands. That's the side of her
people like us see. And fat gratitude she gets for it
sometimes. Like that cousin or sister of hers she
helped. What does she get but the woman coming
here making scenes? She came here once, I wasn't
here. I was out helping Monty get Rommel." He
grinned. "But I remember my wife telling me all
about it. A shocking performance it was."

"I *had* noticed her hands," agreed Ezra.

"She's sharp though. You can't pull the old soldier on her."

He frowned. "Real cross with myself I was. I
ought to have done better." He looked shyly at
Ezra. "You know my little hobby, sir." Ezra did.
The porter had tried very hard to get into the Police Force, and not succeeding on account of his
shortness, had turned himself into an amateur policeman. He had read countless books on criminol-
ogy, kept a card index of famous criminals, with
pictures, in the hope that he might one day meet
one (he never had yet), and kept an alert eye open
for any signs of trouble in his own neighbourhood.
If anyone could be relied upon to notice detail, he
could.

He and Ezra swopped detective stories. Have you
read Ransome's latest? Pretty good you know.
What about the new Punshon? No Daly for a long

time. Is she dead? And the new Innes? Not up to standard.

But now the porter was preoccupied with Dr. Manning herself.

"There's been a shut-up look to the house lately. Doors always closed. Windows up. Not like Dr. Manning. She's nearly always kept them wide open. Like a country woman in that. My wife was a country girl and she always says we don't shut doors so much in the country; me and Dr. Manning we were both brought up on farms. Did you know Dr. Manning had grown up on a farm?" Ezra nodded. He knew about Marion's youth and how she had hated it. Cutting herself off from it had been the first of her big steps forward, the first of her revolutions in transforming herself.

"I didn't like the look of it. Made me think perhaps Dr. Manning was getting nervous of something. I kept a look-out."

"Well?"

"There's been a man hanging about. There were his hands, too, sir. I noticed them. They're wiry hands."

Ezra nodded.

"Then last night. I was passing Dr. Manning's house last night on my way home from the Parks and I saw this man right up inside the garden. He was trying the door, sir, and as I came running up he shook a window. He saw me, I'm afraid, and nipped round the side and off." He paused. "I didn't like the look of it, sir. I'm afraid he may get in. Yes, I'm afraid he may get in."

"He's there now," admitted Ezra. "I've just seen him. And I'm just as worried as you."

"Do you think Dr. Manning's noticed?"

"I wish I knew." He realised that it was important to know if Marion had noticed or not. "I'll talk to her." But it was not going to be so easy for him to talk to Marion; the figure of Rachel stood between them. "But I promise you I'll look after Dr. Manning."

Rachel came hurrying through the glass doors from the library. Ezra got up to help her with the books.

The porter watched them go away. He remained worried.

"Perhaps I ought to have told him. And yet it was only an impression. Still I did *get* the impression: that he was *whispering* to someone inside the house."

THE MAN WALKED DOWN St. John Street, through the crowded Cornmarket, and down St. Ebbes to Pratt's Place where he entered a house which was one of a grubby grey stone terrace. He had a key and let himself into a dark and smelly hall. There was an upright yellow oak hallstand just behind the front door on which lay a few letters and a bottle of milk. He turned the letters over, but there were none for him. He picked up the milk and listened for a few minutes to the noises of the house. He could hear a baby crying and the shriek and scream of his landlady's voice, he could hear someone banging away as if chopping wood, not that anyone ever chopped wood in that house, but banging was a necessary part of life there. After listening for a moment, he went upstairs.

His own room was tidy, dusted and neat. His landlady, oddly enough, had her standards. In her own way she liked her lodger and regarded him as an improvement on the last man, an itinerant seller of leather bags and shoe laces, who had left a few weeks ago, without paying his rent but taking with him her youngest daughter. It was not yet clear which of them would ultimately be the loser on this transaction. To please her present tenant she put an occasional duster round the room and usually made the bed; she had plenty of time in which to work, as he was out a good deal. He had not told her what he worked at, and, tactfully, she had not asked.

The man sat down at a small table by the window and arranged various things on the table before him. He had a yellow packet of photographs, a newspaper cutting, and a carefully tied-up bundle of documents. He opened the packet of photographs and carefully set out a line of photographs almost as if starting a game of Patience. Four cards in a line and one below. They were pictures of women.

He looked at them in silence, then stuffed them back into the packet, which was already greasy and much thumbed, as were the pictures themselves. He put all the things on the table back into the inside pocket of his blue raincoat.

There was a pause while he sat on the bed and drank the bottle of milk to the bottom. Then he got up, opened the drawers of the old chest of drawers and took out a few layers of shirts and underclothings. He packed this into a small suitcase. He looked into the wardrobe, but it was empty. He was wearing his one suit.

He looked round the room, but it was now quite bare of any sign of his presence except for a book by his bed, and this he did not notice.

He went downstairs and knocked on his landlady's door. She opened it at once. She was not pleased to see the suitcase or to hear that her visitor was leaving. She was a large lazy woman of about forty; the only swift thing about her was her

temper, as each of her three successive husbands
had found in turn. She emerged with a cigarette in
her lips and her expensive and bad-tempered Sia-
mese cat clinging to her shoulders. They were both
slightly cross-eyed.

"Well, you'd better come in and talk it over,"
she said, holding the door open. "I can't say I'm
pleased about this, as you led me to believe you'd
be a permanent. I've let slip several good offers,
one very nice undergrad" (this was a complete lie,
no undergraduate would step into her house) "and
one from a very well-to-do lady as would have done
for herself. You've let me down. Well, come on in."

Although the house was dreary enough, the
landlady had created a certain comfort in her own
room. Everything was placed just where it could
contribute most to its owner's comfort. The round
table, perpetually covered in a white and blue check
tablecloth was so placed that it caught both the
warmth from the fire and a good view from the
window. On the table were a newspaper, a radio,
and a box of cigarettes. By the fire was a teapot and
another cat.

"I've kept the cats out of your way, as you said
you hated them. I thought you liked it here," she
said in a hurt voice.

"I'm afraid I have to leave, though," repeated her visitor, his mouth setting in firmer lines than his usual mild expression had led her to expect. She saw this, and abandoned her hopes of getting a month's rent from him. "It's unfair, though," she said, with a genuine sense of grievance. "You'll have to pay up for this week," and she held out a hand.

As he got out the money to pay her, his envelope of photographs fell to the floor. One picture slid out.

"Why, you've got a picture of Dr. Manning," she said in surprise.

"You know her?" Her lodger sounded not too pleased.

"Not half! Used to work there. As a lady help, you know. Just to oblige. But I didn't stick it. Couldn't do with her. Always following me about to see if I worked properly. Looked as frail as a feather, she did, but her energy! Had me beat. All her friends used to say, 'Oh, Marion, I don't know how you do all you do, with your health, and your headaches. You ought to rest more, dear.' Tough as an old boot she is really. See *me* out."

"She's very ill," said the man.

"*Is* she?"

"Very ill."

"D'you mean she's dying?" asked the landlady huskily; in a way she had liked Marion. Anyway she wanted to think of her as in the land of the living. Alive to be grumbled about, not dead to be pitied.

"Yes," said the man slowly. "She will have to die. There's no hope for her."

"How terrible," said the woman; she looked down at the picture and exclaimed: "Why, you've got marks all over the picture. It's all drawn over."

When he had gone she looked after him in disquiet. The effect of the drawing on the photograph had not been pleasant. She was a great newspaper reader and could remember the Heath case and the Rillington Place murders.

"Could be one of these women murderers," she said with a shiver. "I'm better without him."

She turned back, safely, to the comforts of her room, to her teapot, her cats and her cosy fire.

THREE

FOOTSTEPS ARE ALWAYS heard in Chancellor Hyde Street. They are usually the footsteps of people hurrying through; housewives on their way to the Cornmarket, young mothers pushing back from the baby clinic to get lunch on the table. In the evening, the feet are slower; a guest from the St. John's Senior Common Room, coming comfortably homewards, or a late employee from the Clarendon Press in Walton Street wandering home dreaming of the work just done.

Now there were feet that were going very slowly. There was a heaviness to their tread, almost a hesitation, they showed their fatigue. All the same they were feet that knew where they were going, hesitating yes, but always continuing in the same path.

The man had counted however without the inexplicable in life, the unforeseeable chance which sweeps the traveller off his own path and on to another. The moment which could not be predicted had arrived.

He was observed by a neat quiet old gentleman polishing his brass and whistling as he did so. Major Nickols was working on his front door in the house next to Marion's when he heard the feet and at once looked up. He was interested in nearly everything that went on in Chancellor Hyde Street. He had been away on holiday and was just catching up on his household duties and on local events. He knew his neighbour Marion, had raised his hat to her often, and liked her, although he deplored her views on the weeding of her garden. He had even met Joyo, but had retired from her somewhat bashfully.

The Major was a retired Indian Army Officer, a sedate figure, who never mentioned his thirty years in India and hardly thought about them. "There are two sorts of Englishman in India," he used to say, "those on whom India has a profound effect, whose imaginations are completely captured by it and who never get over this feeling, and the others who remain indifferent. I was one of the second sort. I might as well have been in Basingstoke. No imagination I suppose." What he did miss, of course, were the hordes of servants. But even there, he composed himself with the reflection, it had taken three men to clean a pair of shoes and then not as well as he could do it himself. He ran his house quietly and efficiently all on his own, donning a butcher's blue apron to do his chores and

singing quietly to himself as he did so. He had only
one song, the song that had taken his fancy as a
young subaltern years ago, the calling song from
"Rose Marie". He sang it very badly but with feeling. To make ends meet he let one room in his
house to a suitable undergraduate. A young man
who took a room with the Major was lucky, because not only was he well fed (breakfast only) and
beautifully looked after, but he emerged from the
experience with a profound respect for the iron
routine of the British Indian Army. On arriving
there he might have been casual about time, a late
sleeper, careless about his appearance. He never
was when he left. As might be expected, the Major
had had considerable success in the Schools, most
of his lodgers took firsts or good seconds and he
had created one Conservative M.P. and one shy
young Fellow of All Souls, who still returned to the
Major for moral support when life, as it often did,
became too much for them.

Major Nickols looked and saw a man in early
middle age pulled over by a heavy bag and walking
very slowly down towards the last house at the corner of Little Clarendon Street and Chancellor Hyde
Street. This house was a large and shabby lodging-
house.

"Wouldn't have given that fellow any responsibility," thought the Major, rapidly summing up the face. "Still, not quite the sort to live next door if that's what he thinks he's going to do." The Major had a low opinion of next door, where there were great late-night parties, drunkenness and noise. But it was quiet enough now.

He got on with his polishing and watched the man.

The journey from the house in St. Ebbes had been a slow one and the man was painfully tired. He was breathing rapidly and a thick red flush had crept up his neck and over his cheeks.

"Bad heart there I shouldn't wonder," decided the Major. But he was a soldier, he had seen men after battle, overwrought, on the edge of unbalance, teetering towards an explosion, about to maul others and themselves too, and he frowned.

The man rang the bell of the house in Little Clarendon Street. Rang it and rang it again. No answer. He was puzzled. This had not been expected. There was a hole in his plan.

The Major spoke up. "You won't get an answer. No one at home." At ten o'clock the previous night an ambulance had drawn up outside the old house and a stretcher had been carried out bearing the little figure of the old landlady. No more would she enliven the night air with her tipsiness.

The man hesitated. "But I'm going to live there." He spoke in a husky voice.

"Not be able to do that, I'm afraid. Old lady's gone to hospital. Had a stroke. Thrombosis they call it now." The Major prodded at a weed with his foot and glanced, automatically and disapprovingly, at Marion's wilderness.

"Have you come a long way?" he asked.

"Long enough."

The Major saw that the man's clothes were very neat and clean, his white collar spotless but a good deal creased. Did he sleep at all? he asked himself, looking at the darkly shadowed eyes.

He looked down at the man's feet; they were dusty, and the man was lifting them alternately as if they ached.

"They couldn't let you know," he said sympathetically. "Happened so suddenly. Old lady went off last night. Lodgers cleared out this morning. She didn't have many anyway. Been getting dottier and dottier. Still you won't want to hear that."

"I only fixed it up yesterday," said the man.

"Did you indeed?" said the Major, rapidly taking in the significance of that. In that case the man must have been in the neighbourhood yesterday and not, as one might have thought, travelling a long distance. This reinforced his impression there was something rum about this fellow. "Been away myself," he added, "heard all about it from the old lady's cleaner."

"Oh." The man glanced doubtfully up at the house.

"She won't let you in, I'm afraid. Can't really. Old lady took all the keys to hospital. Daresay the police or the fire brigade could do it for you. But 'tisn't as if you'd been living there already, is it? None of your things there?"

The man shook his head.

"Won't do then. Have to try somewhere else. Lots of places," and the Major turned back to his brass door knocker.

He did this deliberately; an old sergeant whose experience included almost all things that can happen to men, had said to him, "If you're doubtful about a man, make an opportunity to turn your back on him and watch him without him knowing. It may be dangerous" (and indeed the Major had once been knocked out while doing it) "but you can learn a lot."

Behind his back there was no sound. For a moment the Major felt a cold apprehension. He knew what that meant.

"Dammit, the fellow's watching *me.*"

He turned gingerly, regretting that in the brass he could see only a blurred distorted image. Indeed, not an image at all, only the impression of movement. But the movement had been one of exhaustion and not of violence; the man was sitting on his case, looking at his feet. His fair hair was clinging to his scalp, and the sun caught the yellow cufflinks.

"Quite a natty little dresser," thought the Major wryly. The figure on the case swayed. Against the background of all his other feelings, a wave of pity rose. He trotted down the garden path and put a hand on the thin shoulder.

"Ever so sorry, sir," mumbled the man.

The Major spoke with sympathy. "You're clean tuckered out." As he spoke he was already gathering up the hat from the ground and the raincoat over one hand, he put a hand under an elbow and hoisted him up. "Better come in with me." He got the case in his hand as well and together the two of them stumbled up the path.

Afterwards, he said, "I'd never have let him in if I'd known, but how could I?" As it was, his white head wagging with sympathy, he put the man in the back bedroom so lately vacated by the last student. It was a corner room with two windows, a man's room full of highly polished dark old wood. A big chest of drawers, a small bed, a thin little rug, spartan yet homely.

"When did you last sleep?" asked the Major, but not expecting an answer. He looked down at his sleeping visitor.

As he went quietly down the stairs to make himself a cup of tea he reflected: "If you can't look after yourself at your age you'll be a fool?"

All the afternoon and on into the evening the man slept, but not dreamlessly, in the narrow borrowed bed. Sometimes he threw out a hand and called.

Down in the kitchen the Major listened and wondered.

WHEN THE VISITOR WOKE he raised himself on one elbow and looked across the room; it was now dark and he could see across the few feet of garden into Marion's sitting-room. Through the lighted window he could see a vignette: Marion, Ezra and Rachel sitting round a table. He could see them outlined clearly against the white walls, and framed in Marion's green and white striped curtains. He could even see the redness of the geranium on the window shelf, but he saw it as a point of brightness against a dark green plant. He could even see that they were at dinner; his own stomach rolled emptily. He looked at them dreamily, sketching a different picture for himself: he was in the room but not with *them* nor was he at meat with them.

Marion, on hearing that Ezra and Rachel wished to talk to her, had firmly asked them to a meal. She knew from experience that good food could assist the most rending emotional discussion. She saw emotion ahead. Rachel and Ezra created for themselves a problem out of Ezra's way of life and Rachel's reaction to it, and in Marion's opinion would involve all their friends in it before they were done. She had summed up Ezra's position accurately enough in her own mind: he was a perpetual scholar; she herself saw nothing dangerous or wrong in this; Rachel did: that was the difference between them.

"Nothing serious before the meal," she said, handing them sherry. And then, "After we've eaten," she said as they sat down at the round table with the long white cloth and the ivy-patterned plates. Let them wait, she thought with amusement, to get at each other.

She was surprised to discover it was herself who was under discussion.

"I'd rather you hadn't worried Rachel with this," she said, frowning. What she meant was "I wish you hadn't let her into our secret."

"Look, Marion, Rachel *knew*," said Ezra, leaning forward. "She saw."

"Oh, did she?" She crumbled her roll on the tablecloth and arranged the breadcrumbs in a pattern. "Well, really, my instinct is to say nothing about this affair. To make nothing of it and to let it be nothing, to let nothing come of it. The man is seen, but I shall pretend he isn't. Then he will go away."

"Oh, don't be so Alice in Wonderland, dear." Ezra was impatient.

"You should go to the police," said Rachel, as dogmatically as if she had not been full of Marion's pigeon casserole.

"What about?" Marion shrugged, and produced cheese and fruit to be eaten on the old painted plates that had belonged to her grandmother. "He's not there now."

"You ought to go to the police. Or else get hold of the man. Ask him. Go on and face whatever it is."

Marion rejected that with scorn. "Only someone who has never been in any danger could say that. You don't rush out and shake hands with it. You hide as long as you can." She peeled an apple carefully. "Besides, have you ever been to the police? No? Well, they've got ways of their own of making you feel a fool.''

"Strange words, coming from a woman of your education and training," commented Ezra.

Marion got out the brandy and smiled.

"There's something unreal about all this conversation," said Ezra, "and it's coming from you!" You of all people, he implied. He thought of all the times he had been with Marion when she had been a rock, a guide to him; the time she had dealt with the young woman who very nearly got Ezra arrested on the Swiss border by making what the young chubby Ezra could tell were most indelicate advances, the time she stood between him and disaster in the shape of the University Proctors when he produced a performance of *Samson Agonistes* with Becky Neumann wearing gold tights and golden high-heeled boots in the University Church and the Vicar accompanied by the Vice-Chancellor walked in, both of them expecting a quietly reverent performance, and got the full glory of Becky's massive but well-proportioned body wobbling along a sort of tight-rope with trumpets sounding and Ezra as Samson baying dismally in the background: the pair of them closely resembling, as looking back Ezra had to admit, two grossly overpainted dolls. Ezra smiled: Becky's day had been a pleasant and amusing one but short: and now she was beguiling the last Maharajah of Lissapore.

"What I can't understand," said Rachel, looking thoughtfully down at her plate, "is it being you and a man, Marion."

"What do you mean?" replied Marion tartly. "Think I look too virginal or something?"

"No," for indeed the word was not one to connect with Marion's fine but battered appearance. Her hair was sometimes such a strange colour that one wondered if she could be dyeing it, except that with Marion one knew she never would. "No. I suppose it's because you've never been married," said Rachel tactfully and relentlessly following her train of thought.

There was a moment's pause. Then:

"I have had a husband once, as a matter of fact," said Marion, as calmly as if she was not throwing a bombshell at them.

"I had no idea," said Ezra, after a stunned pause.

"I know that"—there was a flash of amusement in Marion's eyes. "Oh, well, it was a long time ago. It's no secret particularly, a good many of my own generation know about it, but at the time it was too painful for me to talk about and then later, well, there seemed no point. What was there to say?"

Immediately Ezra remembered what she had said to him earlier: she had seen a man die.

"Yes, he was killed," said Marion. "On that long-ago trip to Central America. At the time I was bitter because I thought he had been killed because some other members of the party had been careless and slack. Now I don't know. Time seems to have blurred the details. I no longer have the same certainty."

"Well, I'm blowed," said Ezra. "And I thought I knew you as well as I knew anyone."

"You shall know everything in future," apologised Marion, looking at him with humorous eyes.

For a moment they paused, considering the picture of this young man falling to his death thirty years ago in the Gran Chaco. I wonder what his name was, thought Ezra. And then he remembered the name of the young man who had died. Funny nothing was made of the fact he was Marion's husband, he thought. To protect Marion, I suppose.

"Francis Eliot," he said aloud.

"Yes." Marion looked towards the wall where there was a snapshot of the whole expedition. "Oh, I expect he would have been intolerable as a husband really as he grew older, and certainly I wasn't much cop as a wife, but it seemed lovely to us then and perhaps if he'd lived I'd have been different."

They looked at each other with the affection and respect that can grow up between two people of different generations but alike in spirit and ways of thinking.

Rachel saw them and a shiver of jealousy ran through her. She put it from her angrily. "I don't *really* care for Ezra," she said to herself.

Marion dismissed them suddenly, with the food still sweet in their mouths. "I have to work." And she put on her great spectacles and looked wistfully at a pile of books and papers.

"You shouldn't eat in the room you work in," said Ezra, as they rose to go. "It's uncivilised."

"I am uncivilised. Didn't you know?"

Rachel strode through Chancellor Hyde Street, she had thrown off her swathed bands for Marion's dinner and was dressed in the green silk dress she naïvely described as her best. Ezra looked at her with his usual mixture of irritation and admiration: any one of his pretty little pupils could have done the dressing better, but without Rachel's poise. "I cannot suppose she buys those clothes," he decided. "They couldn't come ready made. She *retrieves* them somewhere. Or her mother, her grandmother probably, gives them to her." But only his true love could endow them with that air of having been dragged on anyhow and the devil take the hindmost.

"Wait for me," he said, running behind her like a dog that hasn't grasped that it's not coming on *this* walk.

Rachel looked at him silently and, alas, churlishly. If I'm not careful, she told herself, I shall behave like one of those juicy magazine heroines and quarrel so provokingly with my Ezra, biting the hand I really love. But damn it, I don't love that hand. And she looked even more crossly at Ezra's long thin cigarette-stained hand. The hand clasped her firmly just above the elbow.

"I'm worried about Marion."

"I'm worried, too. But don't let's talk about it now. I'm too happy walking along here enjoying the Oxford evening. I love the seediness of Wellington Square, don't you? And you merge so well with it, my love."

In his dark room the watcher stirred in his bed and got up. He saw them go past. He could hear the Major walking carefully up the stairs, he was being quiet but the stairs creaked all the same. He stood up.

Meanwhile Ezra had almost walked himself into the quarrel Rachel had waiting for him.

"At moments like this I know I couldn't leave the dear old place." He gripped Rachel even more tightly. "I'm doing the work I want to do. Quietly delving into texts, long morning's teaching, long afternoons in the Bodleian. And then I've got my acting."

"You're a rotten actor," said Rachel. "And you know it."

"That's not true." Ezra was hurt. "I've come on a lot. All the critics say I speak verse beautifully."

Rachel snorted.

"And my Polonius was praised everywhere."

"Polonius!" said Rachel. "Merely being yourself."

"I don't know why you're being so nasty to me," said Ezra. "I should think you'd be glad I was happy."

"Because I can't bear to see anyone like you wasting yourself, that's why," said Rachel in a rising voice. "*Be* the prototype of the modern wastrel. *Be* the perpetual scholar."

Ezra gripped her shoulders angrily. It was his first step as a man of action, and he was surprised to see how easy it was.

And Rachel's shoulder felt warm and smooth beneath the thin silk; she had very little on underneath it. He realised then why the dress had looked so odd, it was meant to be worn upon a thick stiff foundation of petticoat to hold out the skirt; Rachel had just slipped it on, and over nothing by the feel of it.

"Lovely soft shoulders you've got," he said absently.

"Let go," said Rachel indignantly.

"Don't be silly," said Ezra, and bent his head towards her. He did kiss her, whether it was against her will or not he was never sure, but afterwards they raised their heads and looked at each other like a pair of indignant and bewildered young ponies. Then Rachel kicked Ezra hard and deliberately on the shins.

"Oh, pooh," said Ezra letting her fall back against her door. "The game's not worth the candle." He turned his back on her and strode away. Rachel crept upstairs.

Ezra as he walked home was furiously angry but at the same time pleased with himself. Instinct told him that he had taken a step forward with her. But only if he could stop himself apologising tomorrow.

He passed the Professor of Morphology who was also slowly returning home to North Oxford. He seemed glad of company and talkative.

"I've just been sending off references for a pupil for a scholarship in America." He wagged his head. "They ask such extraordinary things. In your opinion does the candidate adjust well to group activities? Is he likely to make a negative or positive contribution to seminar discussion?" The Professor looked thoughtful, he tried to diminish himself, to slip through a keyhole into a world where group activities and negative and positive seminars really mattered, he found it difficult, but he could just do it. "I always answer yes to everything," he announced.

"And do you have any luck? I mean do any of your students get scholarships?"

"Oh, invariably. I believe they don't read what I put."

An undergraduate cycling past, academic gown flying, nearly knocked him over. The young man stopped, apologised with graceful courtesy, and sped on, very nearly knocking the Professor over again.

"My ideal university," said the Professor dreamily, "would be one without any undergraduates in it. A quiet, scholarly, happy world where one need never see a *young* face again."

"But who would you talk to?"

"Ourselves, of course."

"And what about?"

"Again ourselves."

But Ezra was quite unable to keep off the subject which preoccupied him.

"I never knew till today," he said, "that Marion Manning was married."

"Had been married," said the Professor, his eyes still apprehensively on the cyclist, who was wobbling. "Didn't last long you know. Charming fellow he was."

Ezra made a noise of assent as if he had known.

"Surprising thing that was. Never thought of him as a marrying man."

"Wasn't he young then?" asked Ezra disappointed.

"Lord no. Quiet neat little chap, twenty years older than Marion. Mystery she married him. We could all see what he saw in her though. Great buxom girl she was then," and he gave a deep laugh.

"Don't be coarse," said Ezra coldly. Really, quite a mistake that dons lived remote detached sexless lives. Never forget old Sir Charles Buffon.

"Coarse? My dear Ezra!" and the Professor opened his eyes wide. "Nothing coarse about marriage. You ought to read the marriage service on the causes of matrimony."

"I meant in relation to Marion."

But the Professor had gone back to Marion's marriage. "My goodness, she was sitting on a delayed action bomb there all right," he said almost with satisfaction.

"What do you mean?" asked Ezra, hastily seeing that the Professor was about to disappear. He was like the Cheshire cat and could do it in stages.

"Well, old Francis was a queer cuss. Couldn't tell how he'd really take to marriage. Specially with Marion, a dear girl but a strong character." His head was still visible but his legs had disappeared. "But there it was, they had a few weeks of sheer happiness (and that counts, my dear fellow), and then he went. Perhaps for Marion it was the best thing." He spoke wistfully. "I was in love with her myself a little, all prepared to be sentimental about her when she got back. She soon shattered that. You can't be sentimental about Marion, she's alive, tough, real, it's her great strength. That's where she scores over poor weak shadows like me. Don't *you* make that mistake."

MARION, working away at her books, suddenly looked up and met Joyo's eyes in the gilt looking-glass.

"Hullo. I kept out of the way while you had them with you, although I like to get a look at them. Nice young couple. The girl's quite good-looking."

Joyo hummed a few bars of music.

"Yes, we've met once or twice. That surprise you? Oh, she didn't know who I was. I never say I'm your cousin or anything silly like that. Because it would be silly. Daresay people wouldn't believe it. Not so much alike are we?" She said it complacently.

Next door the watcher was placidly eating his supper.

Joyo began to hum; she was really a very happy woman, but unhappily, if she was happy, Marion was sad: they were ill-assorted companions. However Joyo was kind at heart and she tried, as far as was possible with her own life, to keep Marion happy. So she stopped singing.

"I'll be out for some time," she announced. "I've been out a lot lately." Thank God, she added under her breath.

Ever since the days of the Australian, Joyo had had a slight Australian accent; sometimes she wasn't quite sure herself whether she wasn't perhaps half-Australian. As well as the accent she had tried out a heavy sun-tan make-up and a slight roll to her walk which to her spelt wide open spaces, sheep-runs and horses, but which had really been peculiar to her Australian gallant, a factory worker from Sydney. This was how Joyo built up her character, like a magpie, a scrap here and a scrap there.

Joyo loved meeting people, but living her circumscribed life (which she blamed Marion for), meeting people was just what she didn't do. She had to arrange it.

She joined an Art Group. It was a good class and Joyo, to her pleasure, showed some skill in draughtmanship and drawing from life; the teacher said she had "a strong sense of composition", a quality which Joyo felt she could usually be relied upon to show. So at the beginning of the art course Joyo was happy; she couldn't go regularly, often didn't appear for weeks (Marion's fault again: how she hated Marion when she didn't get out for weeks). But no one seemed to mind. But as the course progressed the teacher said that it was time for their pictures to show their imagination and their experience. This halted Joyo: she had no imagination to speak of, and she was sharp enough to see that if she started drawing upon *her* experiences then some very funny things might pop out.

So she gave up art and turned to cookery. But from this encounter was born Joyo the artist, a creature not making a very frequent appearance but there in the background and giving Joyo much reassurance. She felt it raised her standing.

The cookery class was not really so much her cup of tea; she felt out of place in it, although she suspected it was used by other lonely women as a meeting place, as something to fill in time, and as a substitute for the kitchens and hungry families they didn't have. Probably there were some happy normal women there, but if so she didn't think they stayed; even the instructress had a pinched anxious look of an invalid mother. There were exceptions, of course. At the first class one woman confided in Joyo that she was a spinster about to marry a widower with two young boys. She never appeared again but the idea attracted Joyo; it was an appealing reason for going to cookery lessons, it was a convincing reason, it was such a *right* reason, especially for Joyo who really had no reason at all for going. And after this Joyo was a woman shortly (she was acute enough to leave the actual time scheme vague) to marry a widower with two sons. She even had names for the little boys, John and Peter; the husband remained a submerged figure, which was frankly how she preferred him to be. In fact, if she could have expressed a wish in the matter it would have been that she would rather have had daughters.

She did not make any friends at the class, though, in fact she only ever had one conversation, except with the teacher. The woman working at the next bench spoke to her one afternoon as they gloomily concocted a supper savoury. (Joyo had unavoidably been absent for several weeks so she had missed the breakfast beanfeast, the lunch-time snack, and the tea-time tasties.)

"The food here is what I call fidgety," said the woman; she was tall, grey-haired and certainly looked as though she knew all about cooking. "I came here because I thought it might give me some ideas, I get so bored with my food, but I don't think it has. Not ones I can use, anyway." She sighed as she grated cheese, there was always a good deal of grated cheese in use at this class. "I read a cookery book by a woman writer last night, such a nice cookery book, full of food you'd love to eat, but all needing a good morning's fiddling work, and an empty kitchen, and peace."

Joyo sighed in sympathy, although heaven knew that there was enough emptiness in her life even if not peace.

The woman went on: "I've come to the conclusion that *all* women who write cookery books are either single or else childless women with husbands who only need a good meal every other day or so. *Not* women with families who want feeding, day in and day out, with four square meals a day. You couldn't love food like they do if you saw so much of it." She slapped down a piece of puff pastry. "I tell you, I just long for the day we live on little pills. Four lovely little pills a day. That'll be emancipation. Better than the vote or equal pay. You know what it is, we're archaic about food, cave-men really, it's time we gave our minds to working out an efficient substitute."

"I just love apple pie," said Joyo wistfully.

This woman, too, was never seen again. Off looking for her food substitute probably. And after a bit Joyo gave up the class; no one spoke to her, she didn't like the food, and she couldn't get out very much owing to strained relations with Marion, so there didn't seem a lot of point in going on.

Joyo did not regret the cooking classes. She had spent the war, together with friend Marion, working in the canteen of a large factory and that had been enough for her. Marion could say what she liked but she herself had no high opinion of the dignity of labour; in her opinion it was a phrase used mostly by people who never did any. She considered, too, that Marion had avoided a good deal of the actual kitchen work and foisted it off on to her, Joyo.

What she did regret was having made no friends. Unaware of her own true character as a sort of vampire on other people's spirits, Joyo saw it as all their fault that they did not respond. She had bad luck, was how she put it. Occasionally, in a flash of honesty, Joyo did admit that she found human relationships immensely difficult.

Take her life with Marion, now. At the moment she and Marion were in a bad patch. Joyo was annoyed that Marion was consulting a doctor for her headaches; she considered that Marion was a bit of an old baby. What were a few headaches? They were a nuisance for Marion perhaps, but the truth was that for Joyo they represented an opportunity for escape; they distracted Marion's attention and with Marion's attention off her for a little while she could disport herself as she pleased. So once again their interests clashed. This in itself was nothing new: they had clashed before and they would clash again, as they had done ever since Joyo had read an article in a highly coloured women's magazine about the work and life of the servant of a famous actress, there had been pictures of the woman at work in the kitchen, at the dressing table and in the theatre. Joyo had enjoyed it and at once identified herself with the woman. 'Venetia Stuart's other self' said the magazine, and to Joyo this was just the expression she was looking for. 'Marion Manning's other self.' The phrase had class. The clash between Marion and Joyo was nothing new, but for the first time Joyo began to see that if she found Marion tiresome and in the way then so must Marion find her.

Marion's feeling for Ezra was undoubtedly putting pressure on Marion and making everything altogether much trickier for Joyo. She didn't really want to get in the way of any plans Marion had about Ezra, but she felt she had her own life to consider. And if she didn't consider it no one else was going to. A crisis was blowing up between Ezra and Marion, and nothing that she or anyone else could do was going to stop it. It was in the course of nature and it was going to happen because there was a young girl with a slim waist and a fine skin who had caught Ezra's mind. Marion couldn't hold out against that. Wouldn't want to probably, considered Joyo somewhat scornfully.

For all that, the real Joyo, on whom all the other Joyo's were accretions, had crystallised in the canteen during the war. She had detested much of it, but never again had she found the same freedom. Joyo had loathed the long hours, the dullness, the heavy work of the canteen. "I'm not cut out for this," she used to moan, and hated Marion for it; rightly, no doubt. But she had been excited by the people she met. And like a little girl from the country it had gone to her head and she had let the situation get out of control. One rôle that Joyo could honestly, genuinely have played, was that of the unhappily married woman, and it was the one she was frightened of playing. Joyo, who knew really very little fear, because she had after all, so little to lose, was afraid of that.

At first, during the war, before she had a place of her own, she had lived with Marion. They were only just beginning their relationship with each other then. It had started after the bomb incident, at which they had first met. "If met is the word," thought Joyo with amusement. "Poor old Marion, I suppose she had me coming to her." Just lately for the first time she had been wondering if it was such a help to Marion to have her around as she had previously supposed. Heavens, supposing the woman was being kind to her. That would be a joke all right. Her war-time landlady had certainly not been kind. Joyo could still remember the look on her face, not a nice look at all, and she had shooed Joyo out of her house pretty smartly. Joyo had been aggrieved: "Treated me as if I was a *bad girl.*"

This period had also another significance: Joyo had heard of the phrase 'traumatic experience' (anyone moving in the circle of Marion's friends was bound to do so) and considered that she had had one.

There was a basement store-room beneath the canteen where Joyo worked; it contained sacks of dried food, tins of fruit, vegetables and meat, and all the stuff that could find no home elsewhere. Joyo was obliged by her work to go down there at intervals. She liked it—it was dim, warm and quiet. It was not, however, as solitary and unfrequented as you might have thought at first; other people found it dim, warm and quiet, too. Many times Joyo saw a figure move back into the shadows or quietly close one of the further doors. She kept her own counsel, she was learning, she soon understood that the basement was used for the meetings, assignations, and intrigues that are a part of the life of any large institution, especially in war-time.

Among the frequenters of the basement was a stout red-cheeked young woman whom Joyo identified as being one of the clerks in the Accounting Department; her companion was a much older man whom Joyo did not know. She never did discover who he was, but so many thousands worked in the factory that this was not to be wondered at. She did discover that he was married for she saw him one day with his wife, a woman of Joyo's age and more. She looked a sick woman but perhaps she was only an unhappy one. Then followed a period of a few months when Joyo was not about and when she saw the girl from the Accounts again she was still stout but no longer red-cheeked and there was no more bounce to her. Joyo, sharp-eyed as usual, saw that the man had another companion now.

One day Joyo, descending to the basement to collect a sack of flour found the girl and the man there again. This time there was no fear of them minding her; they were dead. The girl had shot herself and her companion. Guns were not so difficult to come by in 1944, and at point-blank range who could miss?

The man was face downwards on the floor and the girl close by. She was curled on a camp-bed, her head flung back on an old army blanket and her hands free. For the moment there was the quiet, the peace, the dignity even of death.

But soon, if these two were left untouched, then sordidness would creep back; the bodies would stiffen and contract, the features change, the blood darken; the disarranged clothes become disor-

dered and disgraceful. The peace of death is in one
way an illusion; it is only a momentary stage on the
way to disintegration.

It was all a severe shock to Joyo whose own life
was far from tranquil at the time. But it had done
one thing for her: she had seen the girl's face, seen
the look of satisfaction on it, and she had learnt
from it.

From then on she had known that there was one
sure way out.

NEXT DOOR the Watcher sat placidly eating his
supper in the Major's basement dining-room. The
Major, an immensely practical man where his own
comfort was concerned, had long ago decided that
what suited him best in the way of meals was a large
late supper with lots of tea or cocoa to drink. A
light tea followed by a large late supper. Tonight he
and his guest were sitting at a cosy round table eating eggs and chips and drinking cocoa, a drink for
which the Major had a great weakness, and indeed, as made by him, well whisked up and con-
taining a tablespoon of rum, it was both delicious
and sustaining.

Neither was a talkative person and silence suited
them both: the Major because he wanted to ob-

serve his man and the other because he wanted to think.

The visitor looked round the Major's peaceful room, so orderly and unorthodox, just like the Major himself. There were comfortable armchairs drawn up to a table which had been reduced to the right height by the Major himself. There were well-placed lamps, well placed by the Major's standards that is: one directly attached to the back of his chair for reading, another attached to the skirting board by the radio and gramophone so that there need be no fumbling around in the dark for switches and records, and another on a long cord so that it could move anywhere. It was a bachelor's house, planned, comfortable and free. The visitor looked at all this with envy and wistfulness.

On the table were all the books the Major loved most: *Pickwick Papers,* Bacon's Essays, and Kipling. He kept *David Copperfied* upstairs by his bed: no one cried more happily over the spiritual death of little Emily than the Major, although in his heart he disliked the girl and was surprised at Steerforth. There were a few pot plants because the Major had green fingers, and a few flower drawings. There was also a portrait photograph of his great-grandmother which had been taken by Mrs.

Julia Margaret Cameron, that early photographer of genius. He had kept it because he liked Great-Grandma's face.

The man looked at this, and the Major wondered if it was with admiration. But he only said indifferently:

"She must have used a terribly long exposure."

"She did, I believe," said the Major blinking. "Three to seven minutes. How did you know?"

"...Bit out of focus. You can tell she moved, it makes it...softer, somehow. Couldn't get away with it now."

"I can see you know about photography."

The man shrugged. A look which the Major made out as one of sullenness slowly appeared on his face. Somehow it made him seem younger.

"Yes, I am a photographer. I stay in London in the winter. Come down here in the summer to take snaps in the street. You know the sort of thing. Take the picture, give you the card, collect it tomorrow, no obligation to buy. I don't think."

"Really? Didn't know we had them in Oxford. No one's ever stopped me."

"Oh, we shouldn't stop gentlemen like you," said the man with a sign of amusement.

"Only pretty ladies, eh?"

"Babies and dogs. Always go for them first."

There was a silence again between them. Perhaps the man was sorry he had said as much as he had. The Major lit his pipe and smoked placidly.

"Have you got nice neighbours?" said the man looking towards Marion's house; he licked his lips as if they were dry.... Fellow looks damned ill, thought the Major. "I mean friends and all that?"

"We don't always see eye to eye." The Major frowned. "She's not a gardener, you know." And then there had been the other cause for embarrassment. "You know how it is when an old bachelor and a spinster live side by side, people begin to make jokes about them making a match of it. Neither Dr. Manning nor I liked that. Not that I think of marrying. There's only two reasons why an old chap like me marries, one is sex, and there's precious little of that left in me I can tell you, burnt out of me, my dear chap, burnt out of me. The other's for companionship and I shouldn't get that from Dr. Manning. Don't ever believe the tale that scholars are open-minded. Stiff with prejudices. Why, I took the trouble to go into the whole question with her of why we *know* Bacon wrote the plays attributed to that man Shakespeare and she took no notice! Said she didn't care. Didn't care! Not good enough, is it?"

"Thank you for everything," said the man suddenly. "I should get along after supper."

"Yes, perhaps you should," said the Major, who was beginning to think he had better be rid of his odd visitor.

The visitor finished his supper quietly, his thoughts absorbed with the house next door.

He was, almost, in.

FOUR

THE TELEPHONE RANG in the hall next to the room where Rachel was sleeping. She lived when in Oxford in a sort of dormitory attached to her college. She had done so as an undergraduate, for her parents, although living in great comfort in Oxford itself, had turned her from the nest to live like anyone else in college. "So good for you to be independent," they cried. Her parents, like Milton, were continually anxious to Justify the ways of God to Man. Rachel who had once hated it and had objected violently, now clung to her room, as much from habit as anything, but partly because it did indeed represent the independence she was supposed to aim at. Not that her parents were in any other way Miltonic. Her mother was very pretty and lively (she had been a Hansom) and both of them, in their rather dated Bohemianism, were a great worry to Rachel, who never knew whether they were going to turn up broke in Corfù or be run in at San Salvador for not wearing enough beach clothes.

Rachel moved restlessly in bed, snuggling deeper into the blankets, she always slept with only a tip of her nose showing, and ignoring the ringing bell. She turned over, her thoughts swinging towards Ezra in that state between waking and sleeping when fantasies are real; in such dreams Rachel had murdered her father, borne twin-headed monsters, trudged through sanded deserts dragging her feet, and wagged her head solemnly on waking, fully seeing the significance of her dreams, and at once distressed and proud to have such a dark subconscious. Now she and Ezra were swinging hand in hand from garlanded trees with apes and birds of paradise around them. Sleepily she decided that there was something funny there all right; she shuddered to think what her erstwhile subjects the Berboa tribe, who had curious notions about dreams, would have made of it.

Next door, her neighbour, a stalwart geographer of about twenty who was still sitting over her books, reluctantly put down her pen and padded out in her slippers to the telephone. She listened, grunted and put the receiver down. "Wait a minute, I'll get her."

"Hi Rachel," she said sternly from the door. "The 'phone's for you." She looked at Rachel accusingly. She usually did look accusingly at Rachel; the accusation being that she did not take her opportunities: she did not make the best of her looks, her brain, or her young men. The geographer herself had no looks and knew it, but she was determined to take all *her* opportunities, and had already got a good degree, knew more about codfishing than anyone in the country, and was engaged to a young doctor who would certainly become either a Regius Professor of Medicine or else, should he decide to be worldly, extremely well off. She had even, for she had a thoroughly nice nature, fallen in love with him. So between her and Rachel there was a curious friendship, she bullied and Rachel let herself be bullied. Rachel felt the unexpressed reproach and was shy about it. She opened her eyes now, wondering what fresh sins of omission Joan (the geographer was called Joan) had discovered and wanted to remind her of. "It's pretty late for a call," Joan said gruffly. Then she relented. "It's a woman."

Rachel looked at the clock. Twelve-thirty. Not late really by Marion's standards. Only late by hers and the Berboa, they both kept early hours. She knew it was Marion.

She heard Marion's voice, at first faint and far away as though she wasn't holding the telephone near enough. "Please come round to me," Marion said and her voice was urgent. "Come at once. I'm asking you instead of Ezra."

"But why, Marion? What's wrong?"

"He's here." Marion's voice had a little hic-cough in it. "He's in. In the house."

"I'll come Marion. Of course I'll come, but Marion, ring the police, too."

"No I can't do that. I can't do that." Marion's voice was growing far-away again. "I'll tell you why when you come. And why I need a woman."

The line was dead. Rachel turned round to meet Joan's worried eyes.

"You heard?"

"Yes. You can't go out now, Rachel." The rules of the establishment laid down that the women, whether graduates or undergraduates, should be in for the night by twelve-thirty. A night porter was provided to see that this rule was kept.

"I shall have to bribe old Tashkent, I suppose." The night man at the moment was an elderly white Russian known (it was not his real name) as Tash-kent.

"Tashkent is not to be bribed at the moment," Joan reminded her. "Not since Sally Fisher..."

"No need to compare me with Sally Fisher," said Rachel stiffly; in spontaneous reaction to her care-free parents Rachel inclined to primness and propriety; it came natural to her to respect rules, and she would no more have broken one now than she would have gambled. Emergency, however, had spoken to her in Marion's voice and she obeyed it.

Tashkent had been appointed largely on the strength of his monumental, austere and handsome appearance, and the fact that he claimed to have been porter to the last British Ambassador accredited to the Czar. The fact that this would have put him well up to the eighty mark mattered not at all: Tashkent could have been eighty, he could have been a hundred. He was not so respectable as he looked, as generations of undergraduates had discovered.

"Oh well, I shall have to climb in," said Rachel with a sigh. "Or else stay out all night. The way Marion sounded points to the latter."

"I don't know why you let that woman run you," said Joan. "My fiancé says..." But by the set of Rachel's lips she could tell that whatever her fiancé had said was not going to be well received.

Rachel cycled rapidly and nervously down Little Clarendon Street towards Marion. In spite of all her travels she was still frightened of the dark and the street was narrow and badly lit. Her bicycle hissed slightly as she sped along. She turned the corner and saw Marion standing by her gate. She slithered to a stop: her borrowed bicycle had no brakes. As she did so, far away in the distance she heard Christ Church's clock strike the hour, one o'clock.

Marion took her arm. "You've been a long while."

"I was as quick as I could be. I was in bed, Marion." Rachel tried to speak calmly, but inwardly she was shocked, never before had she seen Marion look like this, so flushed, so moved. The absurd thought came to her that what Marion looked above everything was *embarrassed*.

"We won't go into the house, let's stand here for a moment. I'll tell you."

Marion had been working, hardly noticing, so she said, that time had gone so quickly. "I seemed to come round suddenly about ten-thirty to hear a noise," she said. "My head was aching badly." In her room, lit only by the one lamp on her desk, the door and the window faced each other, and there was a mirror hanging over Marion's head in which both were reflected. As she lifted her head from what she was writing, so little done and she had been at it so long, she saw movement in the mirror. Then the movement stopped and she could see a hand, glinting whitely like the underbelly of a fish, and curling away into shadow the flesh of an arm. For a second she did not recognise it for what it was, and then the hand came in at the bottom of the open window and she saw long fingers.

Acting instinctively she turned off the light on her desk and stood as immobile as an animal in fear. Now the only light came from the street lamp outside. She could see the clear and empty silhouette of the window. The intruder had gone. But his hand had been inside.

In the next moment, although she heard no noise, she was aware that the front door had opened. But I locked it, she had time to think. (But how was she to know that since then Joyo had slipped out and come back in again?) She was still standing by the desk, still staring into the gilt-framed mirror. She saw her own face with more make-up on than usual, her hair was in disorder, freed from the tight pins she usually held it back with. She saw at the same minute the door swing forward an inch, then more, and still more. She saw a foot.

The door swung wide.

First a hand, then a foot, like some dreadful backward process of birth. Now the whole man.

What happened afterwards Marion did not clearly remember, she never remembered, big shocks are like that. She remembered vivid isolated incidents. The man himself sitting in her own kitchen on one of her white and red kitchen chairs, she herself standing helplessly looking on from the hall outside. The telephone call to Rachel from the telephone on the stairs, and just before this, her short conversation with the man, and the strange, unexpected, frightening words he had spoken.

She had walked down the path to wait for Rachel, knowing that she was not the same person she had been before she heard those words, that she would never be quite the same person again.

Rachel strode on ahead and into the house. Briskly she turned on all the lights she could find.... Let there be some light in this, somewhere, somehow. All the same she was nervous. There was Marion talking away behind her like a demented thing and there, to be faced in the kitchen, was the man. In spite of the fact that she thought of herself as unimaginative Rachel was in fact an extremely apprehensive and imaginative person and she wished profoundly that Marion had not summoned *her* of all people to deal with the stranger.

"Why not the police, Marion?" she repeated irritably.

Marion halted her rush towards the kitchen. "That's what's so extraordinary, that's why I got you, someone who knows me, a woman, Rachel.

He says he's my husband." She repeated the words. "My husband."

Rachel was taken aback. "What did you say?"

"I said 'my husband is dead', and he laughed, and said 'Dead but won't lie down'."

"Whoever he is, I don't think he can be a very nice man," said Rachel slowly. Or one who likes you very much, she thought to herself.

"Nice is not a word that applies to him," said Marion as if it could not possibly matter. "The only thing is: is he my husband?"

"Don't you know?" asked Rachel cruelly. "Can't you remember?"

Marion looked at her, wide-eyed. Rachel stared back: she was suddenly very conscious of Marion as a woman, she could smell the slight scent of her hair and her skin, feel her warmth and her vitality. The guard around Marion had cracked, she was eager and younger, changed, as if the person she had kept constrained within her had burst forth. "So that is what she is like underneath," thought Rachel. "That is the real Marion. I knew there was another one."

"You don't understand, Rachel, how I feel. You think you do but you don't. You're so *frigid*." People were always saying this of the Boxers, a judgement belied, if you thought about it, by their remarkable fertility.

"Oh, but I'm not," began Rachel and then stopped. What was the good? Marion wouldn't believe her.

Again there was that mixture of embarrassment, and, yes, pleasure, on Marion's face. To her horror she realised that Marion was pleased.

"And that's why I asked you to come, Rachel. He may be just some madman, and then we must get rid of him somehow, without fuss. But supposing it's true? I couldn't treat my own husband like that, could I? But I needed someone here, and I knew only another woman would understand. You do understand?"

Rachel did not answer. She was looking through the kitchen door.

The man was sitting at the table, his hands by his side, leaning back against the high woven cane chair. He had opened his tweed jacket.

There was a girlish flush on her face. "Do you think he could be?" she asked. "Do you think a miracle could have happened. Could it possibly be? My husband come back to me."

"Marion, Marion, what are you saying?" whispered Rachel. "Can't you see that he is dead?"

EZRA WAS NOT ASLEEP either on that strange night; he was sitting at his work-table contemplating the whole corpus of his thesis spread out in nicely typewritten sheets before him; behind were arranged row upon row of books, the authorities he had consulted, would consult and hoped to consult; Ezra was a slow quiet ruminative worker, chewing over his thoughts as contented as a cow. Morning was just as likely to discover him, still one shoe on and one shoe off, having written two words, crossed out three, and discovered some fifty books that must be consulted before he wrote another one, having discovered in addition that his hair needed cutting and that he must buy some new shoes, the exact shade of his new jacket. This was how the years passed, this was Ezra, part of the phenomena of the post-war period, the perpetual student, for whom there can always be raised just enough money from grants and funds for one more year's research: Ezra had on his table pamphlets and application forms for the Henry Hamburger Fund for Advanced Research, the Imperial Trust Fund, and the Lowther Research Scholarship Committee. He had been in his time Senior Scholar, Humphrey Research Fellow, Empire League Travelling Fellow, and temporary Assistant Research Professor at Carog University, U.S.A. (this latter in spite of the splendour of its title had in fact been the humblest and worst paid of the lot, it had come as a surprise to Ezra to discover the very low place in the scale that an Assistant Associate Professor rated in the U.S.), and was at the moment enjoying a Rankheim grant: there seemed no reason why it should ever end. This, of course, was what annoyed Rachel, but for no reason that could honourably be put into words. Basically the reason, which remained suppressed, was that at his age, Ezra should be a *breadwinner*: Ezra, full of idealism, affection, and romantic love, had no idea that the chief barrier to success was her unconscious, but quite accurate belief that he could never support her. The resulting irritation between them was completely misunderstood by both.

Ezra, the perpetual scholar, sat dreaming over his books. At the top of the house his landlady, an elderly philosopher from Somerville, was also dreaming.

Far away over the trees of Park Town and beneath the roof-tops and towers and clocks of Oxford, the Vice-Chancellor, and the Presidents, and the Masters, and the Wardens, and all the slumbering Fellows, dreamt too, of quarrels and friendships, feuds and alliances, work and play.

But between Ezra and his work, and his temper over Rachel, which he had by no means forgotten, there kept intruding a face, the face of the watching man: the stray thought kept picking at him that he knew this man: irritably he refused to take it seriously. The truth was that he had thought about the man so much that his face, a pinched white little face, too, had begun to seem like that of an old friend. But I don't really know him, Ezra assured himself, I don't really; naturally not.

Then he heard himself remarking that the face had not, on the last occasion of his seeing it, been so pale. It had been sunburnt. Because of the open-air job, he said.

And at once he remembered. A picture formed clearly before him. A picture of Oxford in summer. It was early on a June morning, and he was one of a group of five people; three young men and two girls, they were walking along the High arm-in-arm, in full evening dress, and, if Ezra remembered rightly, they were singing.

"Jolly fun," reflected Ezra, even though Rachel would certainly have pointed out to him that he was ten years too old for such undergraduate behaviour; twelve months ago he had not known Rachel and so was not in love and unhappy in his love; but what delicious unhappiness, he decided, he would not part with one precious painful drop.

He could see the swirl of the girls' great bouffant skirts and the way the bow bounced about on Susan Connolly's neat little bottom; he had his arm round her waist. He wondered what had happened to the gay Susan. Married probably, girls always did marry, even the most surprising ones; not that it would have been surprising if Susan married, surprising if she didn't he thought, seeing the way that bow had bounced. They had danced all night in the flower-scented marquees at the House Commemoration Ball with the heat inside so terrific that you mopped your brow, the usual cold wind of an Oxford June nipping the girls' bare shoulders whenever you emerged to drink champagne in the floodlit cloisters. There had also, he seemed to remember, been a gentle drizzle; this, too, was quite the thing at a summer ball. It had not damped their fun. He remembered how they had still been giggling as they emerged for breakfast into a grey cold morning. The few passers-by looked at them with the usual mixture of amusement, tolerance and contempt that the citizens of Oxford reserve for the goings-on of the undergrads, especially after a ball.

A Commemoration Ball is one of the most charming of Oxford occasions and moreover it is an undergraduate occasion which the far grander Encaenia Luncheon for those receiving honorary degrees in June or the occasional garden parties for visiting Royalties or Russian leaders are not. A college reckons to give a ball of this sort once every three years so that every generation of undergraduates can hope to attend at least one in his own college. And it is an important occasion to which you go, if you can, *en grande tenue,* the girls in full billowing ball dresses and the young men in tails. There was even a fashion one year for cummerbunds. After the ball there is breakfast with coffee and bacon and eggs which somehow helps to settle a stomach queasy after a great deal of indifferent champagne. Or instead of breakfast, you can go in a punt on the river Cherwell, a weedy but much loved little stream which runs round North Oxford before draining into the Thames; along the reaches of the Cherwell you can persuade yourself that Oxford is still a rustic city rather than what it is, a city with a lovely ancient heart set in new industrial suburbs.

As they advanced arm-in-arm down the High Street towards the City Church a lean figure had appeared in front of them with a small camera. He was one of those itinerant photographers who haunt Oxford during the tourist season, taking snaps of passers-by, concentrating on children, dogs and young women in sundresses.

This figure had, till now, been faceless. Ezra would have taken an oath that he could not remember, had never even noticed, the photographer's face. But now the face hung before him, as if, thought his theatrical mind, it had been caught in limelight. He could see it in a pale intense light like Banquo's ghost. He could see the pallor, the narrow eyes, the thick lips, and he even smelt, something he had thought obliterated from his memory, the faint odour of garlic coming from those lips.

He had every reason, he thought uneasily, to remember the face. It had all been rather loutish. The trouble was that Anthony, charming, amusing, and well born, *was* a lout and drunk. Ezra supposed they had all been mildly tight, but Anthony was a dangerous lout.

It had started when Susan Connolly gave a shrill little scream of horror at the sight of the camera. Susan, who had a huge dress allowance, a very gay life, and a rakish father who was reputed to have told her he would pay all her debts if she would trade her boy friend. (My Depraved Old Dad, as Susan not unnaturally called her father, was very rich.) Susan who was so well known that her little blunt nose and round eyes were always peering at you out of the pages of the *Tatler* like a pretty pink pig. Susan who although not frightened of Depraved Old Dad was sincerely frightened of her college tutor. "I haven't got permission to go to this ball and stay out all night. I daren't be photographed. I've been threatened with being sent down, and I must stay put to get my degree so that I can go into the Foreign Office." Susan who truly believed her pudgy little paws were destined to mould Anglo-Soviet relations.

This was an invitation to violence not to be resisted by Anthony in his post-Commemorative Champagne mood. With a sweep of the arm he had knocked the camera out of the little man's hand and followed it up with a violent push that sent the photographer stumbling into the gutter. Ezra and the girls made horrified noises and Ezra, shoving Anthony aside, helped the man to his feet. His face was muddy and bleeding and the camera smashed in.

Ezra had apologised repeatedly and emptied his and Anthony's pockets of all the money they contained, and promised to get in touch.

But, of course, he never had. In a way he supposed he had been grateful to pass over the incident. Anthony had gone down and he had never seen any of his companions of that morning again. Shortly afterwards he had met his Rachel, and been born anew.

So the man was a photographer, thought Ezra, moodily, studying his nails. Yes, he had just that right mixture of seediness and brashness.

What was he doing hanging around Marion then? Photographers and Marion just didn't mix.

He remembered the momentary glimpse he had had of the man's eyes as they looked up at him from the gutter, full of anger and dislike.

There had been danger in them.

He got up uneasily.

He was not a great believer in coincidences. In his own work, where they occurred, they were usually the result of an error, and however they started out they usually ended in a trap.

"POOR OLD MARION. Reason must be tottering on its throne," Ezra said sadly to Rachel. All the same he could not help remembering the warning of danger for Marion that had flared in his brain.

"Where is she now?"

"She's gone to see the Principal in College," said Rachel, who was tired and white. "I rang up and got her an appointment. *That woman!*"

"Yes, you'd think in the circumstances she wouldn't insist on protocol," said Ezra sympathetically.

Rachel grunted. She and the Principal had had many a clash, starting from the day when the Principal, who was an old and valued friend of Rachel's mother, firmly led the toddler Rachel to be christened in the College Chapel. Rachel's mother, at times persevering and obstinate in her freedom of mind, had been determined not to shackle her daughter's infant spirit. But she couldn't resist her friend's determination, and Rachel's father was away at the time. However, he would undoubtedly have been immobilised by the necessity to work out how far it was right for him to limit a friend's freedom of action in order to protect an infant's freedom of action.

"Marion went off wearing her best navy blue suit and hat and in a most lamb-like mood. I think she's frightened of that woman. What will she do if the police arrest her?"

"They will do. They must, if she doesn't produce some story."

Rachel shook her head in silence. "If only she'd say something," she burst out, "tell some sort of story. Say he attacked her or something. But she won't."

"Certainly I won't," said a voice from the door. Marion walked wearily over to the sofa, sat down and took a cigarette from the Wedgwood box. "Poor little man. Bad enough to be killed, without having me slander him. He didn't attack me."

"What did you tell the police?"

"What I believe to be the truth," said Marion with dignity. "That he came here to this house by mistake, that I let him in, and then telephoned you because I became frightened."

"So you haven't told them he said he was your husband?"

"Not yet," said Marion, after a pause. "Although I shall probably have to."

They both looked at her and she smiled wryly. "No, you needn't say it. Was he my husband? He wasn't, of course. I don't know why I for one moment thought he could be. Mad, I suppose."

The two women were tired and irritable. Rachel had had an exhausting time: she had telephoned the doctor and police for Marion and then waited with her for them both to arrive. She had not seen the police herself except for a minute or two at the beginning; Marion had been with them for what seemed like hours while she had waited, cold and frightened and bored in the little sitting-room. Afterwards, she realised that Marion had not in fact been with the police all that time, but had crept off to sit by herself in the bedroom. She had found her there in the end, sitting dazed and upright. The excitement, exaltation almost, of the mood in which Rachel had first encountered her had faded and she was defeated. She seemed to have no help to give the police, herself, or anyone. For Marion the dream was gone. It had been idle, ephemeral, dotty, false. She was still reeling from the shock of knowing she could have experienced it at all. The death of the watcher on top of it all was a fact she had not yet really absorbed. Part of her knew it had happened, here, in her own kitchen, but underneath was an incredulous stranger. She did not alter from her incredible story that while she had waited for Rachel to come, someone unknown and unseen had crept into her house and stabbed the visitor.

"But you were abstracted," pointed out Ezra. "Thinking of other things, far away. A lot could have happened without you knowing it."

"I was thinking, yes, but there was never a moment when I didn't know what was going on around me. I saw nothing."

"And heard?"

For a moment Marion looked puzzled, as if she did hear far-away voices. Then she shook her head.

"I heard nothing. Nothing at all," she said in firm tones.

"I don't think the man could have made any noise," said Rachel. "He might not even have known he'd been stabbed. You sometimes don't with stab wounds."

Ezra was despairing. "But he was stabbed. *Someone* did come. Marion, there must have been a minute when your attention wavered, a minute you've forgotten. Only a minute, Marion," he pleaded. "That would do."

But although Marion went whiter still, she rejected with a feverish intensity that there had been even a minute when she had not been herself, and in full command of all her faculties.

She seemed determined to put the rope round her own neck.

"Well, but Marion, it's got to be explained." Rachel was floundering.

"Not by me, though. I've told them what I know happened. His call, my telephone to you. How I waited for you."

"Someone killed him," said Rachel.

"Then they did it while I was waiting for you." Marion lit her cigarette. "God knows why or how."

"It's a little difficult for the police to take that, Marion." Rachel was trying to be careful. "You must see that. As far as they can see there was only you who had the chance. They don't want to attack you, Marion, but can't you see they may have to? Who was there but you?"

"If he attacked you or you panicked, that would only be manslaughter, Marion. You could say that."

"I will not say what is untrue. He did not attack me. If I lost my head it was for other reasons."

"Perhaps you lost your memory?"

But Marion could not be moved.

"Do you know I've had nothing to eat," she said suddenly. "I can't use my kitchen. The police have locked it up. I don't even know if they've left the house."

"They have," said Rachel turning away from the window. "They've left a man in the road though. Naturally. When this news gets out there's going to be quite a crowd round here."

"I hadn't thought of that." Marion's face went even whiter.

"Hadn't you? At the moment I believe the neighbours think maybe you've committed suicide. That's keeping them busy at the moment. They haven't caught on to the fact, the blissful fact, that there's been a murder on their own doorsteps."

"How do you know all this?"

"Do you live in a dream world, Marion? Well, as a matter of fact the Major next door told me. He stopped me in the garden. He knows the truth."

"Oh, that little man. He's a great gossip." Marion sounded disapproving. She and the Major were not twin souls. The garden divided them for one thing, and then Marion, more orthodox than she would admit to, could not get used to the sight of the Major primly pinning out his own underwear.

"He's a very well-informed gossip," Rachel told her. "And as for the food, Marion, you owe him thanks for that. He's sent across a picnic." She pulled a basket in from the hall, and crouched down by it, unpacking. From this point she saw the sitting-room from a new angle, it had a new face, rather as if you suddenly saw an old friend upside down. And several things stood out which had gone unnoticed before. The Meissen shepherdess who was, let's face it, coy and irritating, had been pushed forward, whereas properly she had her face to the wall; and the utterly enchanting but admittedly extremely ugly jade monkey had been obscured by a bunch of artificial flowers. Artificial flowers in Marion's room, who never even looked at a real one! From her position Rachel could also see dust underneath the sofa. It was not surprising that Marion was oblivious to household duties although it was true she was assisted by an odd scarecrow of a woman one saw on the stairs occasionally. Didn't she have the aristocratic name of Mrs. Beaufort? Yes, it certainly was Beaufort, although according to tradition her husband had been an Italian immigrant from Milan. Rachel remembered that Mrs. Beaufort had once been porter in a women's college, an occupation very productive of eccentrics for some reason. She stayed where she was with her head bent over the basket; she had a strong feeling at the moment that she wanted to meet no-one's eyes, especially Marion's, so clear, and Ezra's, so loving and angry. She shook her hair over her eyes like a cross little Skye terrier and peered at the basket. It was well loaded with food wrapped in thick but spotlessly white napkins. "Ham, cheese, hot pastry and coffee. Good for the Major."

"I'll get some cups from somewhere. And some brandy. I need *restoring*." And Marion bustled out, looking much better.

As soon as she had gone Ezra dragged Rachel to her feet away from the basket. He was surprised to find how violence grew upon him and supposed uneasily that he had a taste for it. She smiled at him uncertainly but his eyes were only angry; if there had been love in them then it had gone.

"You believe she did it," said Ezra savagely.

"I haven't said so."

"It's obvious. The way you speak to her. Asking her to admit to an attack." Ezra was curt. "In the way you did."

Rachel did not answer.

"You do hate Marion," said Ezra. "Don't you?"

"I didn't say that either."

"Again no need." He was losing his temper. "It shouts from your manner. And I never knew till now."

Rachel was disconcerted and unhappy. She had had a difficult time and now Ezra was attacking her. Oh fine, she thought, we're getting along splendidly. Nothing like a love affair for making you really beastly to each other.

The police did not arrest Marion. She was saved by her reputation, her good name, and the impossibility, which even the policemen in St. Aldates recognised, of believing that Dr. Marion Manning, scholar and writer, could have killed this little man.

She was cleared also by one other thing. The knife which had killed him had not come from the house.

FIVE

THE DOCTOR MARION had consulted on her headaches was concerned about her. He had sat in the back of the court at the inquest on the dead man and regarded the scene with increasing apprehension.

He watched the behaviour of the police and drew his conclusions. Inevitably, he had gathered in his wandering career a certain understanding of the ways of police and prosecutors, and when he saw how the group of men concerned with the case gave their evidence he was convinced they were keeping a great deal back. Not perhaps of evidence, but of understanding. If you could ask them for their reconstruction of what had happened it would probably turn out later to be an accurate one. It seemed overwhelmingly clear to him that these quiet, patient, and apparently kindly men *knew*.

He observed Marion sitting among her group of friends: Ezra, whom he knew by sight, Rachel whom he had never met, and the head of Marion's college who had come to give her moral support and was plainly failing to provide it. She was

dressed in black from head to foot and even Dr.
Steiner (he was considering anglicising his name),
used as he was to the affection for black of many
continental women, could see that this was wrong.
Marion was not in black but in a sort of tabby
brown which looked as though she had made her
bed in it, as she probably had. Rachel was huddled
in a dark loose coat, and Ezra was wearing sub-
fusc, the decent, dark suit in which he had taken all
his exams and trotted up to receive his two degrees. He was leaning forward to listen and there
was the same look in his eyes as in Marion's, giving him, for the moment, a family resem-
blance.... What a lot, thought the doctor, so
English, so anxious to dress for the occasion and so
perennially uncertain exactly what the occasion is.
A wedding, a funeral, a Peace Conference, a war,
they were never sure whether these were occasions
for amusement, despair, or courage, and met them,
as their clothes reflected, with a triumphant mixture of the lot. Cheered up and reassured by this
apothegm, the doctor went back to watching Marion. She seemed the least concerned of all. She sat
there relaxed and dreamy. Not drugged, as he had
for a moment thought, but dreamy. She had no
headache just now, then: no anxiety about accusa-
tions of murder either. Marion seemed protected by

PLAY THE
LUCKY CARNIVAL WHEEL
GAME ...

GET YOUR
FOUR GIFTS
FREE!

PLAY FOR FREE! NO PURCHASE NECESSARY!

HOW TO PLAY:

1. With a coin, carefully scratch off the 3 gold areas on your Lucky Carnival Wheel. By doing so you have qualified to receive everything revealed—FREE books and a surprise gift—ABSOLUTELY FREE!

2. Send back this card and you'll get brand-new, first-time-in-paperback, Mystery Library™ novels. These books have a cover price of $3.99 each. But THEY ARE TOTALLY FREE; even the shipping will be at our expense!

3. There's no catch. You're under no obligation to buy anything! We charge nothing—ZERO—for your first shipment. And you don't have to make any minimum number of purchases—not even one!

4. The fact is thousands of readers enjoy receiving books by mail from the Mystery Library Reader Service™. They like the convenience of home delivery and they love our great prices!

5. We hope that after receiving your free books you'll want to remain a subscriber. But the choice is yours—to continue or cancel, anytime at all! So why not take us up on our invitation, with no risk of any kind. You'll be glad you did.

No Cost! No Risk!

her assumption that her innocence could never be questioned. He looked at her with liking and affection, for she had been so good to him when he had landed at Oxford, a city over-endowed with refugees, as a battered, shy, and miserable traveller. He had thought of himself as a traveller then, a man with no settled home, but under her patronage (he did not disdain the word) he had built up a little circle of prosperity: he had his flat, his concerts, and his tiny group of friends. She had done all this out of disinterested liking and he thanked her.

He listened with glum concentration to the evidence as it related to the dead man. He had never seen the man and there had been no photographs in the press, but he thought he could have predicted the sort he was. A man destined to be attracted to the person least suited to him, bound to marry a wife who would dislike him in the end. A man fitted out to be destroyed. Someone would surely have killed him, a careless lorry-driver, a bungling surgeon, a clumsy nurse. All the same, he was no doubt attractive to women and some woman somewhere still loved him and thought of him. A mother or sister probably. A man with anxious, timid features, and watchful eyes, although eyes that were very unobservant of what really mattered. A man with no sort of luck whatever.

Meanwhile, he realised he had responsibilities towards Marion who was his patient. He was undecided whether to consult Marion about Joyo or Joyo about Marion; he was acute enough to realise that at bottom it was a problem about their relationship. Superficially Marion was the person to start with, but just lately he had the crazy idea that he might approach Joyo.

He was reluctant to summon Joyo, but it ought to be done.

The truth was that he was frightened. He told himself often that as a doctor he should not be frightened of a woman, and a sick woman at that (for he could diagnose Joyo's sickness). But he had been a prisoner in a concentration camp for upwards of nine years and the button which operated fear was old and easily touched. And then there had been a look in Joyo's eyes on the one fleeting occasion when they had met that had alarmed him. Not, oddly enough, because it had been the cruel look of a tormentor (he had learnt to bear that fear) but because it had been the look of someone about to be tormented.

He was frightened of Joyo, and by her, and with her.

It never struck him that she might be frightened of *him*.

However in this matter Joyo got in first. She consulted him.

She came to call, and planted herself squarely in a chair, with her hands on her knees. She looked agreeable and determined.

He was doubtful how to treat her and decided to leave the interview to her. She had turned up, let her get on with it. With curiosity that in a less searching crisis would have been amused, he wondered how she would play it. Would she be the affectionate friend? the worried old servant? the puzzled innocent?

Joyo was none of these things; she was the Downright Adviser. She knew *Best*. Or so she let her manner imply.

"Marion ought to go away. Right away. For a long time. I suggest a good holiday. You know what I mean."

"She can't go just now," he pointed out. "The police would have something to say."

"That's exactly what I mean. She's in trouble. I wouldn't like to see her in worse."

"I suppose not." He wondered about that though; he had an idea that except for the inconvenience to herself Joyo didn't mind a bit.

"Now you are her doctor. She'll take advice from you. Be obliged to. Send her away. You can do it."

"You think so? You know what you are suggesting?"

"Right away." Joyo was firm. She was in danger of losing the Downright Adviser in the Boss Figure.

"You want to get rid of her?" Automatically his professional eye observed her empurpled cheek and her rapid shallow breathing. A heart swollen to the size of a cow's probably.

"There's not that relationship between us at all," said Joyo stiffly. "We're friends."

"—Liar," commented Dr. Steiner inwardly.

"I know what you're thinking," went on Joyo. "With Marion away, what about me? How would I get on?" She leaned forward. "But that's the point. I'd be all right. I'd stay, you see. I'd look after things for her."

Thinking of Marion's affairs in those muddled hands, he asked: "How about you taking a holiday?"

"Not for me," said Joyo. "I've had them, and never again. I'm never going away again. Let *her* go."

For a moment her eyes wandered round the room. It was a pleasant if inexpensive room and contained many of his little treasures. "He was done in with a knife, you know," she said with apparent inconsequence. "No one knows where it came from, either. I suppose you'd have lots of knives around, you being a doctor?"

"I am a physician not a surgeon," he said stiffly, but he knew a threat when he heard one. There could be nothing in it, he knew there could not. But supposing she endangered his precious little world? Oh God, he told himself, you should steer clear of neurotics, that's the thing about them: they ruin other people's lives besides their own. In that moment he could almost have killed Joyo.

Joyo changed the subject. "You think you know all about Dr. Manning, don't you?"

It was a preposterous question and he answered it coldly: "I only know what she has told me."

Joyo ignored that. She lowered her voice and leaned forward confidentially, "Supposing I told you that there had been a child?"

"My first reaction would be to say this was an untruth," he said phrasing his words with care. He did not wish to alienate this creature. "I would say that it was not true and could not be true." But he grasped that Joyo believed it to be true, believed that Marion had borne a child without her knowing. This belief could explain the monstrous degeneration of their relationship; it could explain Joyo's state of mind, which was getting closer and closer to hatred of Marion. It could not, of course, explain Joyo.

For a second he toyed with the amazing thought that the suggestion might be true. He knew that patients could suppress incredible parts of their lives; the good doctor was never surprised.

"If there was a child," said Joyo, speaking carefully in her turn, "born after the father got killed, a posthumous child, then he could be a young man going about Oxford now."

"I see you have settled the sex of the child," pointed out Dr. Steiner.

"Boy or girl," amended Joyo irritably. "It doesn't matter. But it would explain such a lot." What she meant was that it would explain why she, in spite of her scorn for Marion, yet always felt inferior to her. She did not respect Marion's intellectual achievements, she did not respect her moral standards, but deny it how she would she *did* respect Marion. And there had to be a reason for it.

"It would not explain why she kept it secret."

"Oh you wouldn't have to have explanations from Marion. She's crackers. We all know that."

The enormity, as well as the simplicity, struck Dr. Steiner, but he was strangely touched. "Poor soul," he thought, "poor soul."

She soon dispelled this softer emotion. "Don't you think it would be best all round to send Marion away on a long rest. I know you can fix it." Her round face was earnest and apparently well-intentioned. "I'm not thinking of myself."

"You wouldn't have much money, would you, when Marion went away?"

"I'd get a job," she smiled at him. "You wouldn't like a house-keeper yourself?"

Dr. Steiner grew cold at the suggestion. Was this then what she had been leading up to all along? Joyo in his flat, perpetually there, part of his carefully hoarded and enjoyed life? It was a terrible suggestion. Then he saw she was joking. He hoped it was all joke. Though to be sure, he would have a certain power over Joyo.

"I am my own house-keeper," he said.

"I like you, Doc," she said, as she prepared to go. "And I tell you what, so does Marion." She gave an awful wink.

This time the doctor felt the nerves of his own heart twitch and contract. Joyo could convey so much in an idle phrase. After she had gone he went to the mirror and studied his face.

Could he see there the anxious eyes, the pale lined face which had distinguished the dead man?

Were they then the same type? Sadly he concluded this was so.

He recognised that perhaps he had misunderstood Marion's interest in him from the first. She had not been all that disinterested.

Now he was frightened of Marion, too.

A wave of nausea seized him. He felt sick. He had an ulcer. Or was it something more malignant? He felt very sick indeed.

"I must get away," he moaned.

DR. STEINER WOULD HAVE been even more frightened if he had known what Joyo had in mind. Her appearance in his consulting room, although it had been extremely satisfying to her and had, as she put it to herself, 'gingered him up', had only been a first appearance. She meant to call again. More than once, if she could get in. She did indeed like the doctor, and she knew Marion did, too, but when she next called, she hoped not to find him there. She wanted a quiet time alone in his office. On her call this afternoon she had been carefully noticing where everything was kept, and she had promised herself a splendid time going through his case-records. Not, she asssured herself, out of plain nosiness, although she would certainly take the chance of checking upon the exact age of the nasty woman assistant in the grocery store, and on the *real* cause of the illness of the woman next door but one; but because she wanted to confirm her belief that Marion had borne a child.

By now she had convinced herself that she had heard this somewhere on good authority and if she could only remember exactly who had told her or where, then she would *know*. *Know* was written in great capitals in Joyo's mind and was luminous with meaning. She had for a short time wondered if Ezra was the child in question, but then she decided he was too old. "Too long in the tooth," she had put it vulgarly; a judgement which would have depressed Ezra who prided himself on his young look.

Ezra was shopping at the time when Joyo was calling on the doctor. Joyo was not entirely without justification in what she had wondered about Ezra because he did indeed have a forlorn, unmothered look about him as if he had never known his mother; this was true, he had been told that she had died when he was born and he never thought about it. Had she existed in this world he would certainly have expected to have recognised her at once, to have seen in her features a reflection of his features, in her voice an echo of his voice, to feel the pull of the blood relationship. There was nothing of this feeling with Marion, but perhaps it had been a lack in him which had attracted Marion, not for her motherliness, but for a protectiveness which she was ready to assume and which he had missed in his life. It was possibly this want which bedevilled his relations with Rachel. Unconsciously he demanded much from her.

But Ezra as he shopped was not thinking of Rachel, or Marion, or his mother, or even, for once, of himself. He was thinking about the police. He had noted their behaviour at the inquest and he also had guessed that they knew more than they were prepared to say. He was perturbed about Marion; he had watched her at the inquest with surprised eyes, and instead of admiring her composure, as he might have done, it had only made him cross. He was anxious, Rachel was anxious, so Marion ought to be anxious too. What was more, her indifference to her own plight was downright stupid. Marion ought to care.

He fingered the socks he was buying and matched them up to his tie. "Not my colour," he murmured regretfully. "Got any more?" The assistant produced blood-red nylon and at once Ezra's fluent imagination saw the red of a judge's gown and Marion in the dock. "I won't take the socks," he said, and walked from the shop.

He could see Marion standing there, or did they give the accused person a chair? Anyway he could see her, and himself, as a witness. He would not be far way, for English courts were so small, so cosy, so intimate that you could see the whites of the prisoner's eyes.

Would it be the Central Criminal Court, the Old Bailey as it was often called, or the Oxford Assizes? The Oxford Assizes probably. He had once seen the Assize Judge leaving the Judge's Lodgings in St. Giles; he had watched him walk across the pavement to the car followed by his Marshal and saluted by the policeman on duty; at the gutter the old man had stumbled and Ezra, who was near, had gripped his arm to steady him before being waved away by the Marshal. The car had driven off, and Ezra had been left with the impression that the arm of English law was thin and frail. That week the old man had awarded in a polite sub-acid tone sentences of sharp severity to three louts who had beaten up an old postmaster, sentenced a baby cruelty case to what amounted to life imprisonment and condemned a man to death. The arm might be frail, but it was working.

Was Marion now to be subject to it? Ezra had noticed something at the inquest that Dr. Steiner had missed. The Coroner's Jury had returned an open verdict of murder by person or persons unknown. The Foreman of the jury, an intelligent and kindly Oxford tradesman, was known to Ezra, so he had observed him more closely than he might otherwise have done. He had seen the man's face as Marion gave her evidence (and very badly, too). He had also seen a note passed from the Foreman to the Coroner and back again, he had seen the look of worry on the Foreman's face. He mentioned all this to a lawyer friend. "Oh I suppose he was afraid that they might have to bring in against the woman. Coroner's Juries hate to indict a woman," responded his friend. "It's a known thing. Just like Welsh juries won't convict a woman on a capital charge. But the police were glad to have it left open, you see. Got to get the evidence tidy." Ezra absorbed this in all its implications. "I notice you say 'woman'. You think she's guilty?" "Well, isn't she?" responded his friend easily.

It seemed to Ezra that Marion was already condemned. It was difficult to believe her guilty and yet difficult to believe her innocent either.

Ezra's features drooped, unconsciously he took on the expression of Marion. Perhaps he was like a little dog which has lived too long with one master and they have grown alike.

NOTHING COULD HAVE BEEN more discreet than
Joyo as she crept into the ground-floor surgery be-
longing to Dr. Steiner. She had just missed meeting a policeman, and although she had every faith
in her ability to win over an Oxford policeman used
to the capers of undergraduates, she did not wish
to bother. In her black coat and skirt with her hair
tidy and not too much lipstick she could have been
anyone, even the tutor of a women's college. She
looked kindly and she certainly looked respectable. No policeman would worry about her even if
he saw her climbing through the ground-floor window. She could always say she had lost her key. He
would probably help her in. She had rehearsed what
she would say if the policeman appeared again:
"Oh, constable, do give me a hand, I've stupidly
left my key in my other bag," and provided he did
not smell the breath of Bird and Baby brandy, there
she would be, inside.

She dropped through the window and dusted her
hands which had got grubby in their struggle with
the catch. She didn't rub the dirt off very thoroughly, so that she left a trail of grubby little marks
wherever she touched anything. In the half light she
could not see this.

She grabbed the filing cabinet eagerly. The
thought was rising to the surface of her mind that

she had only invented this theory about the child—no, not entirely invented for surely she had heard it somewhere—but certainly had seized upon it as a reason for ferreting out more facts about Marion. Up to now she could have sworn that she knew everything important that there was to know about Marion; lately this assurance had taken a nasty knock. She had begun to feel that Marion was able to keep a secret from her. Had perhaps always had a secret. "Who'd have thought the old girl capable of it?" she said; she enjoyed talking vulgarly about the unhappy Marion who would certainly never have talked so about her.

What was the secret Marion was keeping? Was it, as she now supposed, the birth of a child all those years ago, when she Joyo hadn't been around? In search of confirmation she went through the filing cabinet. Her speed was reduced at first by the fascination of what she found. Some of the revelations were sad, too, and Joyo, who had a kind heart except where her own interests were concerned had a little weep over the news that the sickness of the lady next door was not, as she had supposed, due to an unwanted child, but to a tumour.

She found a fat docket on Marion, drew it out with a sucking sigh of pleasure, and sat down behind the desk to read it. A good many of the physical details about Marion did not interest her, although one or two surprised and disconcerted her. "What liars doctors are," she grumbled. "Why, old Marion is as strong as a horse. Nothing wrong with her." She paused for a moment at the judgement that Dr. Manning's health seemed at the moment to be comparatively good, except for headaches for which there was found no organic reason. Stress headaches, was the verdict. "And the stress is me," muttered Joyo. Then she went searching on. What she wanted to find out was whether Marion had ever given birth. Surely doctors asked that sort of question? She herself had kept away from doctors but she could remember one occasion in London during her war-time career when she had been medically examined. He had certainly asked her this question and she had given him a black, cold stare and not answered. She discouraged personal questions. Still Marion was just the sort to have answered such a question and truthfully, too.

She was still looking for her evidence when she found something that made her suck her breath in and not pleasurably this time. A little bit of paper was clipped to the bottom card.

The address was ominous: High Elms Private Nursing Home for Nervous Cases.

Even Joyo with her restricted opportunities knew what that meant.

Nor was she under any illusion about who was going there and why. While she had been planning to get rid of Marion, Marion had been planning to get rid of her. And in a downright nasty way.

Great tears welled up in Joyo's eyes. "Beast," she said. "Traitress. And to think of all I've done for her. I hate her now."

SIX

INSPECTOR COFFIN came into the case because of a missing person. Otherwise there was no reason in the world that should bring a detective from south of the river in London to Oxford. He came in search of evidence of his own.

Coffin was a young man for his position as Divisional Detective Inspector even although his Division was small and dingy and unfashionably south of the river. But it was not dingy in his eyes, to him it was a wonderful place full of vigour and entertainment, offering him rich promise for his ambitions; he loved every side street and dirty little alley.

His district had produced one or two original and interesting crimes which had received fair publicity. There was the missing girl from Courcy Street, the Nursery School crime, and already, although Coffin was not to know it yet, there was beginning the stream of events that was to cause the troubled but fascinating crime of The Lottery.

Coffin was a Londoner by birth, from a real old London family, not one of the new ones, come there perhaps from Wales or the Midlands of Scotland in the last generation, but one that had lived in the same district, in much the same way, marrying into the same group of families, since the Great Harry was building in Deptford Dockyard. Such families are as tough, close-knit and localised as village families. They produce people like Coffin: a modern Sam Weller who might have said, in the spirit of his distinguished predecessor, Education: the World; University: Life.

As a detective, Coffin's assets were two: insatiable curiosity and strong common-sense. His life was complicated by a deep liking for people; cautious, hostile, suspicious as a tom-cat at a first meeting, with him to know was in the end to like.

The same river Thames which ran so greenly not far from the Oxford police station at St. Aldates, also lapped, dark and oily and full of dirt, under the windows of Coffin's office in his Division not far from Southwark. Coffin was not thinking of Oxford, but to a certain extent he was under its influence. He was slowly and thoughtfully going through the Catalogue issued with the Teach Yourself Everything Series. (He was doing this in his lunch hour, being a hard-working and conscientious officer.) "Chinese," he said, turning over a page. "Russian, I've tried that but it didn't do.

History, can't see the point; Gardening, too frivolous; supposing I try Anthropology? Learning about people, bound to be a help to me. Give me something to talk about." Not that Coffin ever lacked anything to talk about, he was naturally a non-stop talker, but the subjects which came most readily to him, such as Association Football and Crime, were not always the most suited to the varied audiences he had to meet. He studied the information about anthropology.

Reluctantly he put it aside to get on with the work on hand. He had two missing people reported in his district; one was a woman, and the other a man. The woman, he much suspected, was not missing at all. Or at any rate, not in the sense her husband and family feared. He had no doubt whatever that Mrs. Pearl Meadey was happily ensconced in another home somewhere from which one day she might, or might not, communicate with her husband. She might even return to him. Coffin thought he could put a name to her new home, too; it was reported, although not by her family, who seemed completely unsuspicious ("Noddies to a man," Coffin thought), that she had been seen with Maxie Freak, the little boxer from Red Market; and Coffin knew that it was also said that Maxie had a new girlfriend. No doubt this was Mrs. Meadey, heading for the bright lights. Well, he hoped they suited her, but how, he thought a little sadly, were you to explain to a decent, stupid, worried husband and three small children that mother was away to enjoy herself and would be home if it suited her? No doubt Mr. Meadey would prefer to hear that his wife was in hospital or had lost her memory. Coffin put his problem aside: he would leave it to Mrs. Meadey.

His other missing person was different. The whole episode had been different from anything in his experience, and it was different, too, in the trouble it promised.

This missing person had been reported by his sister. She had really seemed worried, too. Coffin knew Mrs. Good; she was a small hard-working bird-like creature, dark and dusty like a perky Cockney sparrow, and with the same persistent courage. Until now he had not known she had a brother.

"My half-brother really," she corrected him. "I brought him up. As much as anyone did. And though the rest of us had dropped apart we two have always kept together. He lived with me when he was home."

Coffin raised an eyebrow, a query forming on his lips.

"Oh no, Inspector, he's never been inside. Never even deserved it. No, he's a photographer by trade, a nasty chancy business, but he fell into it when he was a young boy. I was always on at him to get a better job. It takes him away from home, down to the coast in summer or to some tourist centre. He's in Oxford Street mostly in the winter."

Coffin placed the brother then, thin-boned and sparrowy and anaemic like his sister but without her bounce. And he didn't look good-tempered either.

"Seen him around," he said.

"Not lately you haven't. He's been away six weeks. But I've heard regularly, cards and one letter. Every Tuesday I heard. Last Tuesday he told me he'd be home on Friday. I waited all Friday but he didn't come. And I haven't heard since. It's a week. I don't like it."

It didn't seem very long to Coffin and he said so.

"It's a long time when you're waiting," she said. "Something's happened to him. I know it has."

"I think you would have heard if he'd had an accident."

"So I would. That's why I'm worried." She had something there, Coffin thought. No news was not always good news.

"You'd better tell me all you know, Mrs. Good."

"He said he was going after his wife." There was a pause while Mrs. Good gathered her thoughts; she did not find it easy to tell a coherent story. "He had a wife. Perhaps you didn't know that. Not many do. She left him. Not that I know anything about it. I didn't know he was married even till he came to me one day and said: 'May, I was hitched last week, wish me luck.' But he was back in a month or two to say she'd gone. And she took with her, just out of nastiness of mind, it couldn't mean anything to her, a photograph he'd made that he hoped to win a competition with. He isn't really a good photographer, poor old boy, but he does try."

She told the story of the marriage. It had been a war-time wedding. In 1944, she thought, at a time when her brother had been working in a London factory and doing only what photography was possible under war-time conditions. A marriage contracted and then quickly broken.

"What was the wife like?"

"I don't know, for I never saw her. But I bet I know what type she was because I know what type poor old Bert always did go for. Bright and noisy and out for fun."

...Just the opposite of you, thought Coffin. Perhaps Albert hadn't loved his sister as much as she'd loved him.

"Well, go on. You know a bit more."

Mrs. Good hesitated. Then it came with a rush. "He saw his photograph in a trade-paper and it had won a prize. There was no name given, at least only a joke one: Fairy. But there was the town it came from, Oxford."

Coffin was doubtful. "I don't know if it's my business to chase a grown man, Mrs. Good. He's free to go off if he wants."

"There's something wrong." Her lips set obstinately.

"You don't know anything of your own knowledge," Coffin pointed out. "Can't take a husband's word on his wife as gospel, Mrs. G. You know that."

"Well, I don't like the sound of the woman all the same," she persisted stolidly. "Besides, I do know something of my own knowledge. I'm not one to leave a thing if I can do it myself. I went round to where they'd been living and had a look. It wasn't the house of a proper woman. I'm not talking about dirt for there wasn't, but it was funny there. And then she'd left everything. Just got up and walked out. Even left a tap running. That was how they found out she'd gone, when the water started flooding down into the landlady's kitchen. And the landlady said . . ." She paused.

"Hearsay again, Mrs. G."

"She said she heard her say, 'I shall have to kill you, destroy you, do you in.'"

"Sharp ears she had, that landlady," observed the sceptical Coffin. "Any other suggestion? Anything else to tell me about your brother?"

She looked round the room before speaking. Then she made up her mind to say what she had to say. "He did hate cats. Gentle as a lamb with anything else but he seemed to feel spiteful to cats. Yet they always made straight for him. I did wonder if perhaps he had harmed a cat in Oxford..." Her voice tailed away.

"Murdered by a cat-lover, eh?" said Coffin, reflecting that she had made her brother sound more and more unattractive with each sentence. A sadistic wife-loser was not his idea of a nice man. "Not likely, is it?"

"He's my young brother. He'd never leave me so long without a card unless he was ill or," her voice quavered, "or worse. I can't just let him go off into the blue like that without making an effort."

"He may not be in Oxford."

"The postmark of his card said Oxford." From her black handbag she produced a grubby bent picture postcard of Carfax, Oxford. There was nothing written on it but the words "Love to all, Bert."

Coffin turned it over. "Well, I think you're making a fuss about nothing. He'll be back."

"I don't like it," persisted Mrs. Good. "I tell you I'm reporting him missing."

"I can get hold of Oxford, I suppose," Coffin sighed. "But don't expect anything to come of it."

"I do so want him back," she said, and her eyes met his. Coffin saw tears in their faded blue, set in her wrinkled, lined and far from clean little face. "He's the only one I've got left." Coffin realised then she was clinging to herself and her memories and the past as much as to her brother, that without him she would slip back into the sea of people without links, without family, who work through the day with no one to go back to, who get no letters and no love.

"I'll do what I can for you, mother," he said from the security of his known world.

"And he's such a silly boy when I'm not with him," she said almost peevishly.

When she had gone he wrote down what she had told him. Missing: Albert Montano, aged thirty-eight. Last seen in London, last heard of in Oxford.

He was unaware then that he was writing Albert's obituary.

COFFIN FOUND HIMSELF still thinking of Mrs. Good and her troubles at the end of the day. He decided to visit the house where this strange couple had lodged. Detectives do not usually have time to indulge their curiosity but this house was not far from his way home, he had a few minutes to spare, and he was interested.

Fifteen years had passed since the whole episode had taken place and this odd little flitting had no doubt long been forgotten in the neighbourhood. It was not likely that the landlady could remember anything about the people even if she was still there.

But she did remember. The moment she opened the door of her house Coffin could see she was the sort who would remember everything that had happened. She was a little London magpie, retentive of everything, memories, grievances, affections, even of dirt. She was still quite young and must have been a very young landlady indeed fifteen years ago.

"Come in," she said in a friendly way without waiting to know what he wanted. "Move along there, Stanley," she said gently. "Don't mind Stanley," she went on. "He's not quite bright, poor little fellow. I look after him for his mum. I haven't none of my own, more's the pity."

"He looks all right."

"Yes, you wouldn't know to look at him, but you'd find out if you saw much of him, Inspector. I'm getting him nice and clean, though. His mum just didn't take the trouble."

"You know who I am?"

"Yes." She seemed surprised. "Don't you know me?" As he shook his head she told him: "I'm Ted Springer's missus. Sent him down for three years, you did."

"Well I never. Don't remember meeting you."

"Oh, Ted always keeps me well away from business," she said, shocked. "Very strait-laced my husband is."

"Yes," said Coffin, reflecting that Ted had gone down for robbing a bank. "Well, I haven't come round about that. Must be nearly out now, mustn't he? Expect he gets full remission of sentence."

"Model prisoner," she said proudly. "He's taken up book-binding this time." She saw that Coffin was looking round the room. "He's left me very comfortable."

Coffin grinned; he knew, and she knew, that the bank had never recovered its ten thousand pounds so that Ted's three years were not without their profit.

He guessed that she would tell everything she knew provided always there was no connection with Ted Springer. She was surprised when she heard what he so wanted to know.

"Fancy you digging that up. I hadn't been married long myself then and Ted was in the Eighth Army. I hardly ever saw him at all. He was out in Africa and then home in time to make D-Day. Never a scratch either, but he went bald, poor fellow. Of course I *do* remember them; they were a funny couple. She was a well-educated woman, though. You could tell it from the way she spoke sometimes. Just a turn of a phrase now and then, but it was there."

He nodded and let her go on.

"Still, she wasn't a lady. Not what I call one. Too loud in her dress and her ways. Of course he liked it. While he *was* liking it, that is. Later on they had some precious quarrels. I used to put the wireless on so I couldn't hear."

"That was decent of you," commented Coffin, thinking of some landladies who would have turned it off so that they *could* hear.

"I could hear even with the wireless on," admitted Nancy Springer. "I heard her talk about killing once." Coffin nodded, remembering what Mrs. Good had said. "But I didn't set much store on it then, although I wondered later when she went off. I don't know if I can tell you much about them. They met in an air raid, so he told me. And it could have been true. Although the blitz was over by then."

"Were they here long?"

She calculated. "About six months, I think. Together that is. He hung on a bit longer."

"Time for you to get to know them?"

"Not really. I didn't try. I was just married myself and a bit dreamy about Ted. I missed him, you see. And then I was out so much. I was a munitions girl. One of the fastest workers they had." There was the echo of an old pride in her voice. "I felt as though I was working for Ted. So we hardly met. When they were happy they were quiet enough. They kept in their own two rooms. We did share the kitchen but you see what with eating in the canteen and being out so much I hardly cooked at all. I think she did a lot of cooking at first, like a kid playing at house, but later on she seemed to lose interest in being domestic, and I think he used to do what tidying up got done, and that wasn't much. She sat around crying."

Mrs. Springer shrugged. "I wondered if he used to beat her, but she had more muscle than him. He wasn't as nice as he looked by a long chalk. Couldn't expect him to be when you think of the district he came from. I know his sister." It was apparent that there had been no love lost between Mrs. Good and Mrs. Springer.

"So do I," admitted Coffin. "She seems all right."

"You know anything about that house of hers in Grindley Road? No? Well, you ought to. Not respectable at all."

"You sure?" said Coffin surprised and interested by this insight into the life of Mrs. Good; he had not suspected it, but now it seemed utterly reasonable. "It's just out of my district, you know."

"Anyway they hadn't been here above six months when off she went. Just scarpered." Mrs. Springer threw out her hands. "It's my belief she was scared of the buzz bombs, they'd just started up. We had a lot round here, as you know. There was one at the end of the road that scared even me and I had my nerve in those days. Remember how we used to talk about 'incidents'? Brings it back, that word, doesn't it? That bomb fell the very day she left because I remember thinking she might have been hit by it. She'd just left the house you see to go shopping. But she was safe enough because she popped back to see if I was all right. She could be kind enough in her way.''

''The bomb dropped the day she disappeared?'' queried Coffin. ''You don't think she was shocked or lost her memory?''

''She was shocked all right, we all were, but her memory hadn't gone. She was quite herself when she went off again. 'Bye-bye, Mrs. Springer,' she said in her cocky way, 'I'll be out some time'. And my God, so she was. I never saw her again.''

''Did it never occur to you that she might have been killed by a bomb?''

''Of course it did. First thing we thought, but you see we got no word and although her husband inquired everywhere he never could hear of anyone that sounded like her. And then he saw her again. On a passing bus. Didn't half give the poor little soul a turn. Perhaps he had made a mistake, but he believed it. He left soon after that. But, do you know, I've heard he is still looking for her.''

''That's right,'' said Coffin, ''so he is.''

''Then he's wasting his time. If she didn't want him, he should leave her alone. I don't know that I'd have wanted him myself, although mind you, he was quite a bit younger than she was. Five or six years, I'd guess.'' She shrugged her shoulders. ''He ought to know better. A woman like that, you can't tell where she comes from or where she goes. It might even be dangerous to follow her.''

"Yes," agreed Coffin. "Frankly, I think it was dangerous. He's disappeared himself now. That's why I'm round to see you."

The woman went white.

She knows something she hasn't told me, thought Coffin, and wondered what it could be.

He looked at her absently. "Did she leave anything behind?''

"Left everything behind her." Stanley and the dog were scuffling round her feet and she bent down so that her face was hidden and Coffin could not see her expression. "He was still here, of course, it wasn't any business of mine.''

"And then shortly after he went off? I suppose he took all his goods and chattels with him?''

She nodded.

"Got anything left?" He removed Stanley from her skirts.

She hesitated, then laughed. "What? After fifteen years? What do you expect? I'm not a good housekeeper, but I'm better than that!''

But Coffin noticed the hesitation.... She's got something, he decided, and wondered how he would get it out of her. Ted Springer's missus must know all there was to know about keeping her mouth shut.

It would be necessary to soften her up in some way, but she had prudently got Stanley back to her skirts and the dog was licking her feet, and she was fussing them in a nice, gentle, feminine way that was impregnable. Also she was murmuring something about a cup of tea being what he wanted.

Coffin accepted defeat; there was no doing anything with a woman as nice as that. He quite saw why the ten thousand pounds had remained with the Springers.

"Put the kettle on, my dear," he said. "I might just as well get something out of this visit. Not your fault, my dear. Don't give it another thought."

She made the tea, gave Stanley a drink of milk, mopped him up, fed the dog, and then sat down.

"Does Ted know?" asked Coffin suddenly.

She blushed. "You don't think I'd keep anything from Ted, do you? Oh I don't mind telling. It's only that I'm a bit ashamed of what I did. Ted didn't know anything about it until he got back and then he took it off me. You could get better ones by then."

"Get what?" Coffin sipped his tea.

"It was a wedding ring." And then, seeing Coffin's look of surprise, she went on. "She left it behind, and it was a twenty-two carat one. During the war you weren't allowed more than eight carat and they didn't look the same, more like brass. And my mum kept criticising mine as though it was my Ted's fault.''

"Couldn't your Ted get you one?'' asked Coffin before he could stop himself.

She faced him reproachfully. "Ted was in the *Army*. He was a good soldier. Never touched a job for five years. He had his stripes and he was keen on the idea. He considered staying in as a Regular, but the pay wasn't what he was used to.''

And Coffin who knew all about Sergeant Springer and his army career, which had indeed been distinguished in its way, nodded. All the energy and intelligence which made Springer outstanding at his chosen peace-time trade had been valuable in the army. For a moment he felt like sighing and saying what a pity he didn't stay straight, and then he remembered the ten thousand and thought that perhaps there was something to be said for Ted's point of view.

"So you took this ring?''

"Not took,'' she corrected gently. "He left it behind when he went. I didn't know how to get hold of him. He took everything else. Even her poor coats and dresses, not that she had many, she went in for those dirndl skirts and dresses. Peasant type. He offered to sell them to me, can you beat that? But I wasn't quite so cold-blooded, besides being thinner."

For a moment Coffin could see the woman who had disappeared—a peasant type, brightly made up, talking a lot, small and sturdy and not quite what she seemed. That was beginning to stand out.

"Got the ring now?"

She nodded. "I kept it. Ted told me to throw it out, but I couldn't."

No, of course you couldn't, thought Coffin, you kept it. No woman could ever throw out a piece of gold.

"Can I see it?"

When it was produced Coffin studied it. It was nothing remarkable. A thick, plain gold ring, not much worn, but not new either. It was the sort of ring his mother had achieved in the nineteen-twenties, not like the eight-carat ring that Nancy had discarded for it, nor like the thin band with orange blossom carved on it that she was now wearing.

"It's an old ring," he said.

"Wasn't the ring she wore every day," volunteered the observant Mrs. Springer.

"Perhaps it was his?"

"If it was his he would have taken it," she said defiantly. "He took everything he knew about."

"All right," said Coffin. "So it was her ring. She had two weddings rings. Lucky girl." He picked it up. "May I take it? I'll give you a receipt."

"You needn't bother. I don't want it back. I wish I'd never touched the thing," and she shuddered.

"You may be right," said Coffin. "You may be right."

SEVEN

IN THE MIDDLE OF OXFORD, at Gloucester Green, stands the bus station used by long-distance buses running from London, the Midlands and the South. The bus station stands arrogantly in the centre of academic Oxford while the railway station is inconveniently and coyly in the suburbs; tradition has it that the nineteenth-century townsmen denied the noisy and dirty railways access to the city. Whether this tradition is true or not, and who is alive now to say if it was so, it is certain that it is a good deal handier to arrive in Oxford by bus than by train; and if you are coming from London you have the advantage of approaching Oxford through its loveliest aspect—over Magdalen Bridge and up the High Street—instead of past the gasworks and the cemetery.

The bus station is lively, noisy, and bewildering. Overlooking it is a small house which is the home of the local Baby Clinic; there are always rows of babies in prams and go-carts, sitting there, tethered, but far from passive, while Mother has a last anxious word with Sister about the extra half-ounce

Suzy *didn't* gain, or the naughty naughty habits of wee William. Next door to the Clinic, very providentially, is a little tea-room where travellers, busmen and mothers find comfort.

Leaning against the window of this restaurant was Rachel. She had spent this fine warm day going back and forth from her rooms to Gloucester Green to meet her mother and father, only to find that her puzzling and distracting parents had never even left Paris. Later she found an apologetic and expensive telegram telling her this and explaining that by delaying another day and a half they could travel excursion and save two pounds; they said nothing about the extra hotel bill which this would let them in for and the brandy and the scent that would get bought, and it had probably not occurred to them.

Rachel shifted wearily on her feet. Then she stared in surprise.

She could see Joyo walking slowly along by the row of prams and staring into each face.

One aspect of Joyo has not received much attention: she was passionately interested in babies; not fond, mark you, or longing, or wistful, but interested. They were strange mystifying little animals to her because her experience had of necessity ruled out any contact with them. She often looked into prams, fascinated by the round, fat, pink faces. If the mother saw her looking, supposedly in admiration, Joyo had noticed there was one comment always made to her. "He's *so* strong-willed." There *may* be parents who think they have got a weak-willed child, if so Joyo never met them. Joyo herself regarded the little creatures with awe, fear and superstition. She would never have actually touched one but she always offered it a nervous proprietory smile. When one cried (and they constantly did cry at the sight of the large, grinning face thrust at them), she took this as a bad omen and hurried on depressed.

Rachel's attitude to babies was quite different; she was a member of a prolific family; she had a married sister and a young brother at the Dragon School (a preparatory school in Oxford) and so she was more matter-of-fact. Insinctively she felt that one day she would be the mother of a family herself and, therefore, must forearm herself with scepticism to avoid sentimentality.

Rachel watched Joyo hanging over a pram. She saw her pick up a rattle and politely return it to the occupant who promptly threw it out again. Joyo picked up the rattle again: obviously this game had been going on for some minutes.

Rachel was considerably surprised to see her.

"Hello," she said doubtfully, adding, "I wasn't sure if it was you."

Joyo was disconcerted to see Rachel, whom she avoided if she could, and as she had better eye-sight than the girl, whose large eyes were very short-sighted, this was not difficult. Her reaction was aggressive; she had heard from Marion that attack was the best form of defence; not by direct exam-ple (on the contrary, Marion was invariably amia-ble and polite), but because Joyo made a point of reversing whatever Marion did.

"You can *see* it's me."

"I don't have my spectacles on."

"Now you're looking at me in a nasty suspi-cious way just like that baby did. Don't *you* burst into tears."

"Perhaps he didn't like you," said Rachel. "Don't wonder," she thought, meeting Joyo's keen cross gaze.

"No, I know what it is. I can see it now, you and he don't trust me."

Rachel shook her head. She was finding it very difficult to make sense of Joyo.

"It's written all over you. Anyway, why were you watching me?"

"I'm meeting my parents."

Joyo laughed. "Where are they? Can't see them." She knew she was being unwise, rash, stupid even, but she could not stop. She was as good as accusing Rachel of being suspicious of her, in her circumstances, the last thing she should do.

Rachel was indeed bristling with suspicion, but the bewildering events of the last weeks had eaten away her usual assurance.

One day she was an ordinary girl (as far as any Boxer could be ordinary) conducting a more or less unsatisfactory love affair.

On the next day she was plunged into mystery, living in a mad, looking-glass land. The only good thing seemed to be that Ezra was turning out to be a stronger character than she had expected.

"I think you are being extraordinary," she said, with as much poise as she could.

"Oh, I don't blame you for being suspicious," replied Joyo. "It's been a funny business all round."

"Still is," said Rachel sharply.

"Exactly. Still is."

"What are you getting at?" asked Rachel in a wondering voice.

"You were at the inquest, you know. The police think that the man was sitting there in the kitchen in Chancellor Hyde Street. Just sitting, when he got stabbed. Ask yourself, is it likely? A grown man, and strong enough, too, sitting there letting himself be stabbed?''

Rachel shrugged.

"No. You can't believe it. But then ask yourself what position he could have been in that would have made him helpless." She paused, then went on: "Supposing he was kissing her?"

"Why should he kiss her?"

"Supposing he *was* her husband. Suppose that!"

There was a pause. Not far away babies were crying, people talking, buses coming and going; all was bustle and noise. But Joyo and Rachel were in a pocket of silence, private to them.

"Why are you telling me this?" asked Rachel eventually.

"Because it is what you think already. It is, isn't it?"

"Yes," said Rachel after a further pause. "Yes."

Without saying goodbye to Joyo, to whom indeed she would have found it difficult to use even the time-hackneyed phrase for farewell (she did not think God *could* be with Joyo), Rachel turned and went away.

But she understood that she could not leave things there, that she would have to go to Chancellor Hyde Street and make one more attempt to get things straight.

If not, then the police. There was really no alternative.

COFFIN DECIDED to go to Oxford himself. He was received by his colleagues at St. Aldates kindly, but naturally with caution. He was a stranger from London, an unknown quantity. The little they had been able to learn by careful and discreet tapping of the only source open to them, had not been reassuring. The source, an elderly superintendent named Winter, already morosely considering retirement, had said: "Very lively. Oh, a lively boy." Uneasily conscious that people touching live wires were liable to get burnt, Oxford resolved to handle him with gloves. So Coffin, bouncing along, half inclined to view his trip to Oxford as holiday, wearing his bright new tweeds (Best Appian Mixture, sir) was stopped half-way. However, he bore himself bravely, used by now to the effect he had on people, although he was always puzzled by the alarm his energy and vitality caused.

"Yes, well, that's the poor little fellow," he said when he had looked at the dead face. "How did it happen?"

"That's something we haven't got quite clear yet," they told him grimly.

"Better ask his wife."

"We didn't know he had one."

"No, you're behind the times. He was looking for her." Coffin told them his story.

"So she stabbed him? Seems a bit arbitrary." Oxford was inclined to be sceptical.

"Oh, you can't tell between husband and wife. Doesn't need to be an obvious motive. Look at the Spens case, and the Wallace murder, and the Fraser dismemberment, all of them husband and wife crimes, and all, as far as an outsider could see, pretty well motiveless. The truth is in a marriage you just can't tell where the rub is, only the toad beneath the harrow knows. Anyway by all accounts she *did* have a motive: she didn't want to be his wife."

"Then it looks as though all we've got to do is find the wife. Want to try it, Coffin? We've only got some thousands of women in Oxford. Not counting the undergraduates, maybe she's one of them."

Before he left they had some information to give him.

"We found out where he lived in Oxford. His landlady came forward and identified him. He'd cleared out the day before the murder. But he'd left a book behind in the room."

"What was it?"

"It was what's known as The Bride's Book. Our Wedding, it said on the cover. Very unusual for the groom to treasure it. But he seems to have been an unusual sort of groom. Or perhaps the bride left it behind. This book is meant to contain photographs."

"And did it contain photographs?" asked Coffin quickly.

"No. It was empty. He *had* some photographs in his pockets when he left though. The landlady saw them. Whether they were from the book or not we do not know."

"Were there photographs on the body?"

"No. By the time we got to him there were no photographs at all."

"My first move will be to go round to Chancellor Hyde Street," said Coffin.

"Nobody there but Dr. Marion Manning and the woman who does her housework," they said.

"Two women," pointed out Coffin, and taking up his new brown-green hat (tones in wonderfully with the tweed, sir), he departed.

He walked up St. Aldates, and towards the crowded Cornmarket, enjoying every minute of the walk.

The crowds thickened at Cornmarket. Coffin found himself part of a steady stream of people all going in one direction, and once in it was not easy to get out. He was wedged in on either side. He found that this stream was bearing through the doors of the biggest Woolworth's he had ever seen. With a desperate effort he clung to the door and turned to face the other way and also the cross, red face of the housewife pushing behind him. "Excuse me, madam," he said squeezing past. He got to the gutter, but not before a piece of vanilla ice-cream had somehow attached itself to his collar. He stood there mopping at the ice-cream and breathing heavily.

"Terrible, isn't it?" said a sympathetic man, picking up his hat for him; it had been badly trampled upon.

"I thought I'd never get out," said Coffin simply.

"I know." There was understanding in the man's voice. "You should never have come in on a Friday if you aren't used to it. Takes practice."

Eventually, Coffin emerged at the end of the crowded Cornmarket into the comparative emptiness of St. Giles. He breathed out. He looked back at the crowd behind him, composed of visitors from America and Scandinavia, town people, country people in for the market, undergraduates, and people down from London and Birmingham for the day, and sighed for the peace and quiet of East London.

He was standing outside the ornate hotel named after Winston Churchill's father, Lord Randolph. In America, or even perhaps in London, such an hotel would have been called, no doubt, the Churchill, but Oxford, with characteristic self-assurance, had named it The Randolph.

An elderly, well-dressed, and beautiful American woman came out of it as Coffin stood there looking.

"You know, Ada," she said to the older, even better-dresssed, but less beautiful woman who was with her, "I can't believe it is good manners to call an hotel by the Christian name of a peer."

"He wasn't a peer, dear," said Ada, who seemed well informed. "Only the son of a duke. It's a courtesy title, nothing really."

"Well, but all the same, it's familiar. They wouldn't have done it with *us*. Now I think I can say that as a family we've had more hotels, hospitals, and centres named after us than any in the States."

"And banks, and railways, and motor cars, and oil wells, and mineral deposits, don't forget, Mar-

garet," reminded her companion. "I always expect your family to do the first real estate deal on
the moon when we eventually get there."

Margaret ignored this. "Except maybe the
Rockefellers, I concede a mite of rivalry there, but
we've been at it longer, but with us it is always the
full name, three initials and all, *never* just the
Christian name."

"No," said Ada firmly, "and since the men in
your family are always called John I can well see it
would not have done."

Fastening their little ties of sable and mink more
firmly round their lovely, if ageing, necks, they
passed on. A group of undergraduates came tum-
bling down the steps after them.

"That's what I like about The Randy," one
shouted. "It makes you feel welcome. I hadn't been
in there for six months, and they *knew* my name..."

"Anyone would know your name, Henry," said
a friend. "You tell them enough. Besides, you're
memorable."

This was true, conceded Coffin. The young man
was six feet tall, with a vast head of red hair.

"They actually knew me," said Henry. "The
porter said 'Hope you'll stay Head of the River, sir'
and he gave me my dinner jacket that I left there the

night Torpids was over last spring. I *am* glad to get it back. I *have* missed it.''

Coffin got out his map of the town and realised he had to walk straight ahead to get to the house he wanted. He walked on, having enjoyed his glimpse of life in Oxford. Indeed, he was enjoying the whole trip. He had discovered the man he was looking for and although he was dead and Coffin had yet to break this news to his sister, he himself was in the best of spirits. He was glad to be on his own; Oxford, thinking no doubt that it had best keep an eye on this stranger from London, had suggested, quite strongly, that it should send a constable with Coffin, but he, even more strongly, had refused. He had his map, he pointed out, and after all no one could ask his questions but himself.

Soon he found the house where Dr. Marion Manning lived without difficulty. He thought it looked a pleasant little place, although he raised his eyebrows at the garden. He saw a curtain move in the house next door. ''Some old woman watching,'' he thought. The Major replaced the curtain and moved back further into his room. Another policeman. Well, it would be interesting to see what change this one got out of next door; the Major had been watching events there with interest since the murder. (He had, of course, told the police all *he* knew, but it did not seem to have helped them much, or if it had then they hadn't said so.) He watched Coffin ring the bell again. "I'll be surprised if she even opens it," he told himself. You couldn't see everything from his house; but with a spy-glass, and the Major had some excellent binoculars, you could see a great deal. "You'd think she had two heads, really you would," he said to himself. "Or is she trying to disguise herself?"

Coffin rang the bell for a third time and this time he leaned on it and did not move until he heard feet; he knew as well as the Major did that someone was at home. He could *smell* someone was at home, he could hear faint sounds.

Presently the door did open, in an irritable kind of way as if the opener wished the caller to the devil. This was roughly true.

Inspector Coffin saw Joyo, although, of course, he did not know this at the time; what he saw was a woman with fierce brown eyes and wildly waving hair who stood before him with arms crossed and feet stockily apart as if daring him to cross the threshold.

"There's no one at home," she announced sourly, and as it happened, untruthfully.

Joyo was alarmed at the sight of Coffin; the full awfulness of what she had done was beginning to come home to her; further, she realised intuitively and at once, that Coffin was the first person she had met so far who would pierce her mystery. And she saw this because Coffin had kind eyes and regarded her with interest and understanding, not with irritation and scorn as so often happened; she feared understanding and interest like death.

"Dr. Manning?"

"She's out," said Joyo fiercely; she would not help this man by one degree; he could see far too sharply for himself as it was.

"Is there anyone else at home?"

"No one lives here except Dr. Manning."

"And the woman who helps her in the house?" said Coffin, who had been briefed by his Oxford colleagues. "Is that you?"

"Yes," said Joyo, after a pause; she resented this summing-up of her appearance; she *did* help Marion in the house, but she was more, much more. "We are close friends. I help her out." The lie meant nothing to her, she told it cheerfully: it would take a psychologist to distinguish between what was true and false in that anyway, she thought with amusement.

Coffin was puzzled by this woman; from her looks she was a rather violently coloured specimen of the type he often met penny plain in his own district, the working woman, independent and friendless. The dead man's sister had not been unlike her. This coloured mask was stupid and cross, and yet, behind it, Coffin could swear he saw intelligence and apprehension. All the same she was blocking him in a stupid way: she must know he *could* get hold of Dr. Marion Manning if he wanted to, could find out all he really chose to, and she could not really hope to stop him. Why try? Unless she was frightened. He sighed; he was too experienced to equate fear with guilt. Some of the most innocent souls were also the most frightened, but fear made his job immeasurably harder.

He could hardly say to her that the murdered man had been identified and that he had come round to satisfy himself whether it was possible that Marion Manning could have been his wife, but that was, of course, why he had come.

"I just wanted to have a word with Dr. Manning," he said.

He set himself to soothe Joyo. But as he did so he became aware of an antagonism that puzzled him. This woman had a chip on her shoulder. While he talked he tried to remember if the local police had

had any sort of brush with her, but they had hardly mentioned her, had scarcely seen her. He put the thought away for reference.

It was just as well he had something put away to think about because with a sudden movement Joyo shut the door in his face.

Too many doors had been shut in Coffin's face for this to anger him. He thought he would play a trick on Joyo. He had already noticed that the backs of this group of houses could be seen from the corner of Little Clarendon Street. He went into the hardware shop on the corner and asked if he could watch from one of their back windows. This was behaviour which would not perhaps win him the thanks of his colleagues but he hoped they would never need to know of it.

He sat down on a box in a room used for the storage of oil stoves, lamps and cookers. It contained also more old chests of drawers than he had ever before seen in one room; these were used as receptacles for nails and screws and bolts. Coffin looked out of the window. Unlike the Major, he had no binoculars with him, but he had an excellent pair of eyes of his own. And to a certain extent he knew what he was watching for; he had recognised the smell which had come through the door of Marion's house. It had been the smell of burning.

Now his interested and observant eyes saw that in that garden where nobody ever did any gardening, someone, presumably the strange Mrs. Beaufort, and how ill the name suited her, was having a bonfire. A nice quiet domestic bonfire.

He wondered what she was burning. Not, he trusted, her employer.

Even as he watched he saw Joyo stagger forward to the fire with a great armful of weeds.

The Major was waiting for Coffin as he reappeared. The binoculars had spotted more than the behaviour of Joyo, and he had seen the detective disappear into the shop. He raised his hat politely (the Major was perhaps the last man in Oxford to wear a hat) as he stopped Coffin. "Decent sort," he was thinking, "make a good N.C.O. In a war probably end up a Brigadier. Not old enough for the last one though."

"Good morning," said Coffin. "Saw you at the window, didn't I?"

"I dare say," said the Major, in no way discomfited. "Good observation post, you know. Now I take it you were wanting Dr. Manning?"

"I was wanting anyone I could get."

"I don't usually interfere in my neighbours' affairs," said the Major, which was completely untrue, as it was as natural as breathing for him to interfere with and dominate whoever came within his orbit.

"But I could see you trying to get in next door. As you saw, I live next door to Dr. Manning."

"Oh, yes," Coffin was rapidly recalling all he had been told of the eccentric next door who had befriended the murdered man. "The woman shut the door in my face."

"I detest that woman," said the Major sharply. "I'm a plain man and I've said it! I detest her. It was bad enough when we only saw her occasionally, but now she's there all the time. She's come to stay if you ask me. I knew there was trouble when Dr. Manning started refusing to go out. I could always tell in the old days with the horses (I was a cavalry man, of course) when you got a horse who kept its head down, wouldn't look you in the eye and stayed in its stall, then you knew you were in for it." The Major spoke in the voice of the confirmed animal lover.

"Mrs. Beaufort is it?" Coffin was considering the possibility that perhaps the detestable Mrs. Beaufort was his girl of the golden ways who had come out of the blue to love, to disappear, and then reappear only with a knife. "Is it Mrs. Beaufort?"

"She calls herself Mrs. Beaufort, does she?" The Major was adding up *his* thoughts and what they added up to was that he didn't believe in Mrs. Beaufort. "An undesirable woman. I should follow her up."

"I shall if I can. Know where she lives when she isn't here?"

The Major shrugged. He thoroughly disbelieved in Mrs. Beaufort. "It's Box and Cox if you ask me, my dear fellow, Box and Cox. But I don't pretend to know. I'm not a friend of Dr. Manning's."

"I could do with meeting a friend of Dr. Manning's," said Coffin, who found the Major quite as remarkable as Mrs. Beaufort. "Or even just getting a good look at Dr. Manning."

"I suggest you get hold of Mr. Ezra Barton. He knows more about her than I do. Close friends. I can give you his address." And the Major consulted his diary.

"You'd be useful to me on my job," said Coffin admiringly. "Talk about well-informed."

"12A Landover Road, just behind the University Park," said the Major, passing over what Coffin had to say.

Ezra, however, was wondering if he *was* a close friend of Marion's. Marion seemed to have withdrawn herself. He reproached himself for having been so sunk in his own affairs lately that he had not noticed Marion. Looking back he wondered whether, as his star had declined, so another star was in the ascendant. There was some influence on Marion that he could not account for. The word withdrawn was not used by mistake: she had gone away.

Just for the moment at the inquest, at which she had appeared most extraordinarily dressed even for Marion, who chose her clothes as eclectically as her conversation, he had got contact with a Marion he understood. He had pressed her arm and said something about thank goodness it was over, these last days must have been difficult for her, and she had looked surprised and said "But I've been *working*," as if nothing and no-one in the world could really impinge upon that.

Perhaps he was wrong: Marion hadn't changed; he had.

All the same it was getting more and more difficult actually to *find* Marion. He hadn't seen her for days. And he missed her. She was good company and he had been used to find her welcoming whenever he called. There was a thrust and parry in conversation with Marion that stimulated. Of course, you could say he got that with Rachel, but with Rachel at the moment there was more cut than parry, and if Marion was stimulating, life with Rachel was apt to be like wearing a hair shirt. They had had a good resounding, heartening quarrel over Rachel's attitude to Marion and although officially it was over, they were still rather tentative with each other as a result. It had shaken them up and neither of them was quite sure yet where the pieces had come down. One thing was clear, they did not stand quite where they had before. Whether Ezra had gone back a move or forward he was not clear. How maddening to have to think of a love affair like a game of chess, that came of Rachel being so tiresomely cerebral: although lately he had been having encouraging signs that she was not entirely mind. He wondered whether Marion, who after all had a mind, too, was being remote with him on purpose. But all his knowledge of Marion, her warmth, generosity, even her good sense, told him this was nonsense. Whatever was happening to Marion, it was not calculation.

"I'm worried," he said to Rachel over coffee in the dark little coffee shop smelling of soup and fish in Oxford Market. "Where is Marion?"

"You could ask her pupils."

"She's not teaching this term. You know that. Working on that book."

"Ask around. At college."

"But I don't want to seem to be *inquiring* about Marion. Things are tricky enough as it is without me adding to it."

Rachel nodded and stirred her coffee. Her own conscience was not quite easy on that count. How much had she added to whatever burden Marion was carrying?

"I just want that one of us should see her. Reliably, actually see her so that we know she's there and not dead or ill or something." Ezra's voice trailed away.

"I have seen her, though," said Rachel slowly.

"What!"

"Yes, don't look so surprised. I've thought all along you were getting over-imaginative about this disappearance of Marion's. I just went round. I wasn't invited or anything. I called. The door was open and I went in. That's Marion exactly. Every door always wide open. No wonder people wander in and get murdered."

"She was there?"

Rachel nodded. "Of course. I've told you all along that's not the worry, Marion disappearing. All the same she wasn't herself. I saw what you meant. She acted almost as if she didn't know me. Or care much either. I suppose she could see I was watching her. 'Don't stare,' she said. Sharply, too. And she wasn't pleased I'd called, either. I'm afraid she hasn't forgiven me for trying to get you out of Oxford.''

. . . Or for as good as telling her you thought she was a murderer, was what was at the back of both their minds.

''All the same she was kind. You know Marion, she'd be kind to you even if she was hating your eyes. She gave me some coffee. She makes rotten coffee, too.''

''So everything was all right?''

''I wouldn't say that,'' said Rachel. She was puzzled. ''Marion looked ill. And thin. She's very thin, I wonder if she bothers to eat? No, there was something odd. I wish I could put my finger on it.''

She brooded into her coffee which she had not drunk, no one ever saw Rachel actually finish a cup of coffee. She started it, stirred it, looked at it, treasured it apparently, but never finished a cup.

''We're not Marion's only friends,'' she said suddenly. ''Nor her oldest. There's Lloyd Farmiloe. They were on the expedition together. I believe they didn't speak to each other for years after it, but he knows her.''

Ezra got up. "Bus or taxi?" he said, knowing how far into North Oxford was the home of the Professor of Morphology.

"Oh, walk," said Rachel. "I always walk everywhere in Oxford."

"You're too good to be true, my girl."

To Ezra it was delicious to be walking into the green shadowy streets of North Oxford with Rachel. This side of the city, far away from the industry and factories of Cowley, was more attractive than people allowed. He liked the large shabby houses, the green lawns and the trees which were at their best in early summer.

They had no difficulty in finding the home of the Professor of Morphology; they heard it even before they saw it.

"Do you think he keeps a zoo?" Ezra turned to Rachel. "I'm sure I've heard noises like that in the Lion House in Regent's Park."

"I *think* it's only children," but she sounded doubtful.

They stood on their toes and peered over the shaggy, sweet-smelling hedge.

Rachel giggled. "I think they *are* children."

In the garden a procession of strange, grubby figures staggered round chanting and beating a dustbin lid. The size varied, the leader was quite tall and, if a child, was probably aged about ten. The last in the line could hardly walk and seemed to be crying. No faces were to be seen, as each head was covered with either a fur mask or a paper mask or dust and feathers. Everyone was very dirty. On another dustbin lid there were the remains of a picnic meal: a pot of jam, a jar of peanut butter, a loaf of very dark stone-ground-no-artificial-fertiliser health-bread, and the chewed remains of a tin of corned beef.

Crouched in one corner by a rose bush was a dark, cross boy of about thirteen, who was reading and trying to type on a small machine placed on the ground beside him. In another corner was a pram, the occupant of which was wailing fiercely. No one took any notice.

The leader of the procession, who was wearing a fur and what was clearly his mother's best flow-ered hat, stopped in front of the boy who was reading and screamed.

Rather nervously, Rachel and Ezra entered the garden.

"Is your father at home?" Ezra asked the read-ing boy politely.

The reader stood up and shook his head. He also was polite. The rest of the children stood around in a large and vaguely hostile circle. "No, he and my mother are both out."

"Is anyone home?"

"There's us," pointed out the leader of the procession. "We're home all right."

At this point, the youngest marcher in the procession sat down and wailed desolately that it wanted its lunch. The baby in the pram abruptly fell silent, unconscious probably.

Rachel and Ezra looked round them helplessly, anxious for retreat but unwilling to abandon the situation without doing anything about it.

"It's not lunch time yet, is it?" asked Rachel. "Surely it can't be."

"It is for us," said the leader of the marchers. "We had breakfast at six so Mum and Dad could get off."

"Perhaps I could cut you a piece of bread," said Rachel, going toward the dustbin lid.

"You can't, we've lost the knife."

From across the low garden fence they had been watched by a pretty blonde woman with big blue eyes.

"I know how you feel," she said. "Imagine how I feel living next door. I itch to tidy up and organise."

By now the marchers were standing around the bin tearing lumps of the bread and spooning the jam. The boy had gone back to his book and the baby was crying again. Rachel found this a relief; she had been so frightened it was dead.

"They do have an Italian," murmured the woman. "Fred," and she called to the boy with the book. "Where's Maria?"

The boy shrugged. "She got in a temper because Jackson left the bath tap running all night, and she's gone off."

The pretty blonde muttered under her breath.

"But what are their parents thinking of," cried Rachel, scandalised, "leaving all this lot with just one Italian?"

"Oh, it's not their *fault*," said the pretty woman regretfully and earnestly, "I don't believe I'd get so angry if I thought it was. They try, they really do. They just can't help it. They're just natural born muddlers." She called to the biggest boy. "Fred, that's your telephone ringing, do go and answer it." When he had gone she said, "He's only home for a few days, he's in his first term at Eton. He can't *stand* the others. I think he's ashamed of them."

"Humourless boy," said Ezra, looking at the dirty, messy, tired, but good-looking and attractive faces before him.

"Yes, they are rather sweet, aren't they? But don't be hard on him, he just wants to be ordinary."

"Yes, I can see this family is different. It must take real intellect to get in a muddle of this dimension."

"Do you know," said the pretty blonde girl, whom they could now see to be pregnant, "every single one of these children is named after a different historical figure. Fred, who's just gone in, is Frederic Barbarossa, the girl is Bloody Mary, the baby is called Alaric. Would you believe it? And every single one of them brilliantly clever." She sighed. "I'm so afraid I'll have a dull little pudding."

The toddler was wailing again, a high desolate cry that made both Rachel and the woman look at each other in alarm.

"I'm afraid that child is an arrant exhibitionist, damn him," said Bloody Mary in what was clearly an exact reproduction of her mother's tones and speech.

The adults looked at each other again.

"I'm going to be obstinately, terribly, relentlessly sweet and polite to my children," said the pretty woman. "So that they can never repeat anything dreadful I say."

"I shouldn't think you'd have much difficulty," said Ezra; he admired her.

The child wailed again so Rachel went over and picked him up. He was fiercely hot and his hands were dry, he was trembling.

"He ought to go to bed."

"I don't think I can climb over," said the pretty woman apologetically, "not as things are."

"No. I'll do it."

"Well, I can take the baby," and she put a pink arm over and lifted the wailing infant from its pram. "Practice for me," she said with a wink, and departed.

Rachel lifted the toddler over the stream of water which still lay on the doorstep and disappeared. Ezra sat in the sun and waited.

When she came back she looked worried, and quiet.

"We needn't have come," said Ezra getting up. "Shouldn't have probably."

"I'm glad we did. That child needed attention." She walked out of the gate and Ezra followed her. "Besides, it wasn't entirely wasted." She walked on ahead without saying anything, indeed she walked until Ezra touched her arm. "You were saying?" he inquired.

"When I had to put the child to bed, and what a mess, it must take real brain power to create disorder of that calibre, I saw an empty photograph frame in the hall. It had contained a group photograph of that miserable expedition to Central America. It said so underneath. I asked the eldest boy where it was. He told me the police had taken it."

"The police?"

"Yes, the police, just think that one over. And whose face were they looking for? The husband's or Marion's? You can take your pick."

Suddenly Rachel shivered.

"You don't look too good yourself."

"Oh, it's nothing, I have a bit of a headache." But she looked pale. Ezra said so.

"Oh, be quiet."

"You're very irritable anyway." Ezra now was genuinely concerned; he had also a feeling of grievance, not only was Rachel being irritable but he was also certain she was keeping something from him.

"I'm not in the least cross," and as if to prove this Rachel switched at once to a subject which never failed to make both of them cross: Ezra the perpetual scholar. Why wasn't Ezra doing something about it?

"You haven't got very far with *your* business," she said.

"Only far enough to make myself miserable and Marion, too."

"You told Marion? No wonder she hates the sight of us both." Hadn't Ezra realised that Marion's interest in him was not entirely that of a mother or a teacher? Obviously he hadn't. Not that, poor Marion, there would ever be any significant development in such a relationship, but all the same she would not relish the sight of her young supplanter.

What with this, and the murder as well, no wonder Marion looked odd. She was such a dear person, too. Rachel thought of that short, stocky figure with a sudden rush of affection.

The sight of Ezra loping hungrily along by her side drove fondness away.

"You must get out," she said sharply. "It's not doing you any good. You're declining. Oh, it's not the place... for the right people it's the best in the world. Heaven knows it's done well enough by my family (all my families you might say). Someone like my Uncle Tim is exactly right here, it brings out his best and he does the best work that's in him. He's a scholar. But you are not a scholar. You can't *think*."

"Thanks," said Ezra.

"Oh, you have force all right. But it's emotional force."

"I'm glad you recognise it," said Ezra, trying to look dangerous.

"And don't try to continue on that line either. It won't work for either of us. Hopeless situation for you to be dominated by your wife."

"You might find marriage changed that, Rachel."

"You're not really trying," said Rachel, persisting in her main object. "We must go at it in a different way. Each morning you must say to yourself, 'Every day, in every way, I am trying to get away.'"

"All right," said Ezra to humour her. But the truth was that, despite Rachel, he was *not* trying. He was quite satisfied as he was, he could go on like it for years.

Thus rationalising away their fears, pushing the half-world of pain and fear behind them, because after all they were young and in love, they walked on. But they had only pushed it behind them, and it was close enough to some people, the lost and the lonely.

Ezra met his old friend, the Producer, within a few yards of parting from Rachel.

Ezra could see at once that he had news value; no one mentioned the murder and Marion, but the thought was there pricking away at the back of the conversation. Unluckily, Ezra did not enjoy it; what was happening was real to him and Marion, almost real, although not quite, to Rachel, who was protected to a certain extent by her native background, and not real at all to the Producer and his friends who saw it as an interesting play in which they happened to know the principal characters. Indeed the *only* characters as far as Ezra could see, for no one had yet succeeded in dragging in from the wings any other character who could share the increasingly ominous doom which Ezra was beginning to feel now attached to him and the others. There was a murderer somewhere and Ezra very much hoped that in the eyes of the police he was a character they had not yet met and not one of those already assembled on the stage.

The Producer was in the company of a charming, well-dressed and not young lady; she seemed familiar and beamed upon Ezra, not perhaps as if she knew him but as if she expected to be known.

"Have lunch with us?" suggested the Producer amiably.

Ezra studied the lady, she was wearing a thin fine wool black suit with a large real spray of lily-of-the-valley, and her hat was entirely composed as far as he could see of those charming flowers. There was a lovely smell, too, of lily-of-the-valley, lovely and larger than life. Larger than life. Of course.

The lady waved away two girls with books.

"No autographs, dears, not just now, try tomorrow night."

"This is Venetia Stuart," said the Producer hurriedly.

"Opening in *Vanishing Point* in its pre-London tour," said the lady, waving a hand at the theatre behind her. "I'm rather afraid its name does not belie it."

"I knew you at once," declared Ezra.

Another girl with an autograph-book hovered near.

"No, dear," said Venetia, "No. I'm not Edith Evans nor Sybil Thorndike. They'll be thinking I'm Mrs. Patrick Campbell next."

"Do you think they've ever heard of her."

"I suppose not," and she sighed. "A lovely actress, dears, and she didn't do half the things they say she did, but she did do some of them. I remember once when I was in the same play with her, and you have to remember I was *very* young, my first pro' part really, and she made such jokes under her breath all the time that we could hardly keep a straight face, and it was such a solemn play, too, almost as bad as the one I'm in now. My dears, if this play staggers to London I for one shall be surprised, such jokes: they wouldn't make a cat laugh.''

But the Producer knew that Venetia was famous for being gloomy about the plays she was in and was confident that her play would run for months and years.

They lunched at a table in the George, a table near a window box full of geraniums, with the punka going overhead because it had unexpectedly turned warm.

"I always have the same lunch whenever I come here," announced Venetia, in full rich ringing tones. "Fried sole and trifle."

"You don't look like a trifle eater," observed Ezra, "more like a smoked salmon and savoury eater."

"What nice things you say," responded Venetia, and she leaned across and beamed at him. There was a warm scented wave of lily-of-the-valley mixed with Arpège. At the back of this, deep down and far away, Ezra was aware of another smell, something faintly medicinal and disinfectant, as if the lady had been having a bath in dettol. With Venetia this seemed unlikely.

"Venetia is going to help me audition this afternoon for the play I'm doing in the autumn," said the Producer quickly, feeling that his lunch party was ignoring him.

"I'm looking forward to it. I adore that lovely dark panelled room of yours with the window overlooking that gloomy old quad, I always feel it looks like the executioners' quad in the Tower of London. And then you will give me tea afterwards. Perhaps we shall have luck, perhaps discover some genius. I'm sure all the young things look at one as if one ought to think so."

The Producer sighed. "Oh dear, they *all* think they are Richard Burtons now and, of course, always one thinks that one is perhaps going to discover another one. I never have yet, I must say."

Venetia leaned forward. "By the way, dears, which of us can that very pleasant young man in the tweed suit sitting over there eating soup be following?"

Three heads turned to regard the man, who swallowed his soup uncomfortably.

"Oh, but is he?" asked the Producer.

"I've been followed before." Venetia smiled wickedly. And indeed she had been. "But at the moment I am behaving with great rectitude. Oh well, there was a small thing, but that was months ago, three anyway, who would be bothering about that?'' She leaned forward and more lily-of-the-valley and Arpège breathed over Ezra. ''I know what you're thinking, young man, 'she's sixty if she's a day', but let me tell you that has nothing whatever to do with it.''

''Oh, I wasn't,'' protested Ezra. At this moment Ezra identified the medicinal smell as being a rheumatic rub much used by his father. So lumbago was the reason for Venetia's rectitude. Venetia could make lumbago fascinating, but even she could find it impeding.

''Yes, you were, you have a very expressive face, but never mind, it's a nice face. But this is no help in deciding who is being followed. Is it you, John dear? No, it's not you, and it's not me, so it must be you,'' and she turned to Ezra. Then an idea came to her. ''Let's call him over. I like his face, I really do.'' She waved an imperious white hand. He didn't move though.

''I don't believe he is a detective,'' murmured the Producer uneasily; Ezra kept quiet.

''Nonsense, of course he is.'' Venetia walked towards him. ''Handsome boy, isn't he, in a tough sort of way?'' Whatever she said when she got there the watchers saw a thick wave of red sweep over the man's face. All the same he looked pleased, and when Venetia returned she had her victim behind her.

Coffin was as surprised as anyone to find himself suddenly lunching with Venetia Stuart.

"You know, there's something familiar about your face," said Venetia as she led him along. "We've never met, have we? No, I could never have forgotten you and those shoulders, dear. I have it, of course, I knew your mother when we were both kicking up our heels at the Old Lyric. I *knew* those shoulders."

"I never heard Mother was on the stage," said Coffin weakly.

"Certainly, dear, isn't that odd, I haven't thought about your mother for thirty-five years and now I can see her as clear as I can see you? She couldn't dance, dear, but she had glorious legs. They were her ruin really."

"Eh?"

"Yes, just as I was saying, you see, no-one minded if she could dance or not, she just had to stand there and everyone admired those legs. Mine were so awful, dear, like barrels, that I was more or less obliged to learn to act, and you see in the long run it paid better. Still, I haven't got a nice son like you, have I?" and she smiled up at him. "Here is Mr. Coffin, boys," and she pushed forward Inspector Coffin, now for ever identified as the son of an old friend. "I was in the chorus at the Lyric with his mother."

They were now a table of four, Venetia sat back, satisfied, and Ezra thought she had probably forgotten why she had set off after Coffin in the first place. But this was not so.

"And now we are absolutely longing for you to tell us why you are watching Mr. Barton," she said. So she knew all the time, thought Ezra.

"He's come about the murder," Ezra heard himself say in unexpectedly loud tones.

Coffin closed his eyes in horror. In his part of the world people didn't come out and shout that sort of thing, but Venetia only looked gratified. There was no doubt about it, she liked a good line. She turned almost in congratulation to Ezra. "Go on, sweet," she said. "Have it out with him."

"It's true enough I was wanting to see you to have a word," said Coffin politely. "And I have been following you waiting for my opportunity. I came after you just after you and the young lady set off on your walk to visit that house with all the children, but it's not true I've come about the murder. Not my case you know, I'm not local."

"London," observed Venetia, spooning up her trifle. "I seem to remember that your mother married a Londoner."

"What have you come about?" asked Ezra.

"I suppose you could say I've come to satisfy my curiosity," said Coffin. "I've got about six hours to do it in because I've got to get back to London today."

"And what are you curious about?" asked Ezra. Venetia nodded, not a bad line at all, no doubt they were building up to a climax of some sort.

"I'm curious about a woman," said Coffin slowly. "A woman who loved and married and went away. I want to see if I can find her. It's incidental to me really if she turns out to be a murderer."

"I don't think that's at all a proper attitude," said Venetia who had finished her trifle. "Not at all what I should expect from a son of your mother. You ought to mind."

"I've told you: it's not my case."

"Oh pooh, who cares about that."

The Producer stirred uneasily. He could see his audition with Venetia (and frankly he had been looking forward to it: surely he could not have misinterpreted those looks Venetia had been giving him?) vanishing into thin air.

"Just for once," said Coffin, conscious that he had a telling line, "I have an academic interest in murder."

Venetia gave a hoot of laughter. Even so she managed to retain her elegance.

"I could fancy some cheese," she said.

"You have the appetite of a cobra," said the Producer without rancour.

"I'm not omnivorous though," she said. "I have my tastes," and she fluttered her long, false, but undeservingly attractive eyelashes at Coffin. He grinned. Ten years in a noisy and vividly alive district just south of the Thames had introduced him to many women similar to Venetia; they may not have had her polish but they had her impulses. While Ezra and the Producer were enchanted by the glamour and gaiety and beauty of the stage star, Coffin saw beneath the Paris hat and the skilful cosmetics to the face of the ageing and lovable woman underneath, but all of them perhaps missed the third and deepest Venetia, the shrewd, relentless, intelligent, slightly vulgar woman who had given success and life and vitality to all the other Venetias who flourished on the surface.

"If there's a woman in this," said Venetia, suddenly serious, "then take some advice from me."

"Yes, there is a woman," said Coffin sombrely. "You might say this case is all woman. A woman came to tell me a man was missing; another woman was there when he died; and a third probably killed him."

Marion must know more than she's said, thought Ezra suddenly, I'm a fool not to have forced it out of her.

Coffin told them all he knew of the case. He was not telling them anything that was not public knowledge although probably Venetia was not aware of this.

"You say you are looking for a woman," she said. "You describe her, only as she was described to you, mark you. Let me tell you you might as well forget that description. You don't really have any idea what she looks like. Women have not one appearance but many."

"I've had one good look at her," said Coffin obstinately. "I'd know her again."

Venetia leaned forward. Her great eyes were fixed hypnotically on Coffin, he was all her audience, and so he got the full powers of a personality that could fill Drury Lane. "You're mistaken," she said. "I don't believe you've ever really seen her, not as she really is."

"We don't seem to know anything then, do we?" asked Coffin spreading his hands. "When is Mrs. Beaufort not Mrs. Beaufort? Quite like a nursery riddle, isn't it?"

Venetia pounced. "Beaufort? Improbable name, isn't it?"

"She's a remarkable woman," said Coffin, when the party separated. "I wonder what she is underneath all that?"

"Pretty tough I should think," said Ezra. "Did you see what she ate? Would you mind if we stopped at this chemist's for a moment. I seem to have indigestion."

Coffin laughed.

"All very well for you to laugh. You know exactly who is under suspicion by the local police."

"To hear them talk," said Coffin, "you wouldn't think they suspected anybody."

"They came and took a photograph from Professor Farmiloe's house," said Ezra wretchedly. He told Coffin all about it, he found it easy, alarmingly easy to talk.

Coffin raised his eyebrows. Nothing had been said about this to him by his cautious colleagues; he was interested, it told him a good deal of what was going on in their minds. It was the way his own mind was working.

"Would you take me to see the Professor?"

"I will if I can, of course. If we can find him. Fortunately he is a man of regular ways." Ezra looked at his watch. "If this is a normal day, and heaven knows if it is, then we ought to find him in his college, St. Mat's." This was the day-to-day name of the famous college of St. Matthew and St. Mark, founded, or so its Fellows liked to believe, by Adam Zouche, a famous money-lender and warlock of the twelfth century. If their claim had been a true one then it would have made them the oldest college in Oxford and humbled the pride of Balliol and Merton. Unluckily it was difficult to prove and it seemed more likely that the college had slid into the world, unobtrusively, in the sixteenth century.

"Now which spot is actually the University?" said Coffin looking around him.

"People always find Oxford difficult to understand. You know during the war the Germans drew up a map of Oxford and put an X just by the Bodleian Library to mark what they thought was the University. There are a few administrative offices there, but it's no more. The colleges are the University. It has no real existence outside."

They walked under a gateway, out of light into darkness, out of noise of traffic and voices into quiet.

"Nice place," said Coffin appreciatively.

"Oh it is," answered Ezra, "one of my very favourites." He thought of all the happy times he had had there. Had he stayed too long? Did they think of him as a little dog they had around the place? A dog they had to pat a little and be nice to?

A small, plump little man came round the corner talking loudly to his companion who was tall, lugubrious, thin. He was complaining in no uncertain terms about the High Servitor, that official college servant who superintends the college wine.

"How can we have Lady Pinckney to lunch with Love pouring the claret all over the place?" he worried. "He drinks, you know, that's his trouble, and what's more he doesn't like us to. Do you know what he said to me last night? That's your third glass of Madeira, Mr. Bristow, and that's quite enough. Cheek, you know. I ought to get him sacked."

Ezra remembered the number of times Love's kindly but trembling hand had dribbled port or claret or hock over his head and into his lap and smiled: how many times had he seen Love angrily scolded and angrily replying (for he allowed himself much latitude in dealing with his employers, rather like an elderly nanny). But however many times he gave or was given notice, Love was always there in the morning again, tottering around.

"Dons always complain about their servants," he explained to Coffin. "They like it that way, but they keep them as long as they can, always complaining, of course, but when they retire they complain even more about the new one and say they don't get the service from him they got from his predecessor. It'll be the same with Love."

As well as the wine, he remembered the very real kindness he himself had experienced once from Love when he had been unhappy and it was clear that he was unhappy.

"We were looking for professor Farmiloe," said Ezra, putting his head in a small window in the porter's lodge.

The Professor, however, was not to be seen. Or rather they did see him, just in the distance, running hard.

"Got to get home," said the lodge porter sympathetically. "Trouble at home."

Ezra nodded.

"He left a note for you, though," said the porter, feeling in a pigeon-hole.

Ezra opened it. *Dear Barton* (they were not on Christian name terms and never would be), *thank you for putting the child to bed which I*

*gather you and Miss Boxer did. I had just
driven my wife off to catch the train for the
Neuro-Philosophical Conference at which, as
you probably know, she is reading a paper. I
had intended to go to see Marion Manning;
from all I hear it is clear that once again she
needs help. You understand? But, of course,
we are both old friends. Go and call on her,
there's a good fellow. She needs help. If you
can't find Marion, ask for the short middle-
aged woman with the dyed hair and the loud
voice.*

He added in a scribble: *Please God you get to
Marion. I'm afraid she is in trouble again.*

Ezra handed this note to Coffin: it succeeded in
at once puzzling and alarming.

"I'd better go I suppose," he said.

"Yes," said Coffin absently. "*You* look for Dr.
Manning. And *I* will look for the other one."

John Coffin, making a polite farewell call at St.
Aldates before returning home, received a piece of
information. Afterwards it occurred to him that
they had known all along.

The murder knife had been traced.

It had come from the Mocha Mecca Café down
by the station.

It had gone from the café just about the same time as one of the customers; neither had so far been seen since.

They did not know her name, but they could describe her. She was middle-aged, plump, much made-up and with a high voice.

"The spitting image of my Mrs. Beaufort," said Coffin. His colleagues watched him with interested speculative eyes. They were not indifferent to what he did, but they thought they would wait and see.

EIGHT

EZRA DID NOT GO in search of Marion as he had
planned. He was suddenly filled with a new and
unexpected anxiety.

For these were the hours when Rachel sickened.

His first warning of what lay before him was a
telephone call from the girl Joan. She sounded
anxious.

"You'd better come round," she said, and afterwards it seemed to Ezra that there was a note of
hysteria in her usually calm, even phlegmatic voice.
"Someone had better come. Rachel's ill. I've called
the doctor."

"What?" said Ezra; he found himself too startled to talk good sense, and yet he had noticed
Rachel's face when he had left her, he had noticed
the flushed cheeks with yet a line of pallor round
the eyes. Why hadn't he realised then that she was
sick?

"I found her when I got back from lunch; she'd
been ill some time then, Ezra, I was rather late
back, I'd been working in the library, it was almost
tea time...." Her voice faded away, and there were

distant sounds across the line, sounds that Ezra did not like. The clink of metal on metal, then a grating noise, followed by the noise of quiet voices. He heard Joan say: "Oh God." Then he could hear nothing more. The receiver was down.

By the time he got to where Rachel lived, Joan was standing limply in the doorway. She looked at him silently.

"Where's Rachel?"

"You're too late."

He went white and leaned against the door.

"No, no, I didn't mean that." She was concerned. "She's gone to hospital. She's alive. Or she was when they left," she added sombrely. "It's no joke, Ezra. Whatever she's got is something horrible. It seems to be eating into her."

They went upstairs to the quiet dark little room where Joan did her work. There was a photograph of her betrothed on the table and he smiled down happily upon the room. Ezra found that he kept catching his eye.

"I thought she was drunk at first because her voice was so thick, stupid of me. Rachel never drinks and anyway why should she so early in the day?" Sin for Joan started at six in the evening. At any other time Ezra would have smiled. He knew well enough that if Rachel had wanted to start the day with neat whisky she would certainly have done so, but the fact was Rachel didn't in the least care for drink. "But then I saw it was fever: her face was so red and she was breathing so oddly. And her eyes, her poor eyes.... Her eyes seemed so fixed." The words reminded Ezra unpleasantly of something Marion had said: "I saw a man with his eyes crossed in death."

From next door came the noise of scrubbing and the sound of water being poured.

"What's that?" he asked sharply.

Joan looked away; she was the sort of girl who always did look away in moments of crisis. "They have to tidy up; there was a mess."

More than anything else this brought home to Ezra that his fastidious beloved clumsily-dressed Rachel was ravaged by a sickness beyond her control.

"She wasn't really conscious," said Joan quickly. "Not by then."

There was a moment of silence.

"We shall have to let her parents know."

"I've done that. But they're abroad. Isn't there someone in England?"

Ezra thought. "There's a gran or something in Gloucestershire."

Two women in overalls came along the corridor. They looked at the two people standing there but said nothing, except that at the door one woman turned back and gave Ezra a smile.

"No good standing here," he said. "I shall go to the hospital." Then he saw Joan's face. "I think you'd better come with me and have some brandy to drink."

"You can't go to the hospital smelling of brandy."

"I can't think of any better place to go smelling of brandy," said Ezra grimly.

But before giving her the brandy he telephoned the hospital from a box in the broad street of St. Giles. Cars were rushing past, but he did not see them, all he could see was Rachel in a high white hospital bed.

He was there in the box for some time while people came and went at the end of the telephone. Then a doctor spoke to him.

"If you are a friend of Miss Boxer's then I'd be glad to see you."

Ezra hurried, completely forgetting Joan still waiting patiently for her brandy, but even so by the time he got to the hospital the doctor was waiting in the entrance hall. Even Ezra, hurried, anxious, preoccupied, could sense the tension that lay behind this waiting. Doctors wait on patients, not on patients' friends. There was a mystery, and the mystery, he knew at once, was Rachel's illness.

An illness like this one, he realised, does not spring forward without a cause, there is a background to it. What had been in the background? Days of nervous strain and worry; looking back with the eyes of knowledge he could see that Rachel had been tense and curiously apprehensive for days now.

"I'd like to ask you a few questions. Has Miss Boxer seemed normal lately?"

"Normal? I think so." But had she? Had any of the three been normal? Could you expect it?

The doctor looked perplexed. "I might as well be frank with you; we are having some difficulty in making a diagnosis. If you have been in close touch with Miss Boxer" (for a second Ezra had time to speculate that Joan had not been incommunicative; that behind the prim manner she habitually got across just what she wanted to say), "then any details you can give me would be helpful."

But Ezra had none to give.

"Certain symptoms: the fever, the violent headache, the vomiting and the giddiness, followed as it has been by stupor, hint toward a tentative diagnosis."

Ezra looked up expectantly and at the same time with dread. The doctor tapped on the table before him (they were talking in a tiny little waiting-room almost fully occupied by a large deal table, its top polished by many anxious waiting hands), but he did not meet Ezra's eyes. He murmured what sounded like 'cerebromeningitis'.

Ezra must have made some sound because the doctor looked up and said hastily, "It's not always fatal now, you know, not with the new drugs."

This was obviously meant to be a cheering statement.

"All the same, certain symptoms are not atypical." He looked down at the table again and did not tell Ezra what those were. In a moment Ezra knew why. "And she is not responding to our treatment." He sounded both irritated and anxious.

"That's it," thought Ezra, "there's the rub, patients *ought* to respond."

"Has she been in contact with any known cases of serious illness?"

"No... That is, there was a child. But that was only this afternoon."

The doctor considered. "Too close in time, probably. But if they had both been in contact with a common source of infection"—he was thinking aloud. "I'd better have the name and address," he said briskly, and having got it, disappeared.

Ezra sat alone in the little room and listened to the noises outside; somewhere under the same roof was Rachel, but he felt no comfort from any sense of contact with her, rather the reverse, as if the world divided them.

After a time the doctor returned. "Nothing wrong with the child. Or not much. Just showing off."

"That's what his mother thought," said Ezra wretchedly.

The doctor tapped his fingers. If I saw much of him, this chap with his tapping fingers would irritate me, thought Ezra. "Can't you *do* something."

"We're not doing *nothing,* you know. Already we've alleviated..."

"And cured?"

"We can't do any more until we get the results of certain tests." He paused by the door. "Why don't you go off home?"

"I shan't go home." Ezra added defiantly, "I'm ill, too." He had a lunatic idea that if he were ill and with the same illness he might get closer to Rachel.

The doctor looked at him. "No, you're not ill. But you can stay." He shut the door quietly behind him. They were all quiet in this place, thought Ezra, that is each individually was quiet but the whole added up to a gentle murmur of noise that never stopped. It was the noise of people living, of people trying to live, and of people dying.

All night the fever raged. But by now it was nothing to Rachel who if she was conscious of it at all was only so in a far-off distant way as if she was a stranger to her own body. Through it, she was weighed down by a sense of doom; aware of very little, she was still aware that she was very ill.

By this time they had diagnosed what was wrong with Rachel but it began to look as if it was too late.

NINE

COFFIN HAD FOUND Mrs. Beaufort, or he thought he had. At least he had found her house, and once again he was standing outside a shut front door, ringing a bell. They seemed to give themselves all the time in the world to answer bells in Oxford, he considered. He was something of an expert in doors, as all policemen get to be; he knew when a door was locked because of fear, because of absence, or because the person behind it was dead. He hoped this wasn't a case of the latter.

Mrs. Beaufort lived above a junk shop in the Cowley Road, which is one of the great main roads leading out of Oxford to London. Her front door was directly next to the door of the shop.

Coffin rang again, this time leaning on the bell with his shoulders. No one came.

Eventually the owner of the shop took pity on him, and poked out a bespectacled face.

"Don't think she's home. Haven't seen her come in."

"She might have got past without you seeing." There was not much hope in Coffin's voice; he could see that the owner of the shop had sharp eyes reinforced by powerful spectacles. And in fact the man ignored his remark.

"Unless, of course, she's *been* in all this time and didn't go out after lunch as per usual."

"Does she usually go out?"

"Sure thing. Goes out to do her shopping. Does charing in the morning." All this time he had been studying Coffin. "What are you this time? Healthy Foods? Nature-Life Scientist? League of Seekers into Yogi?"

"Takes things up, does she?" asked Coffin amused.

"A real old crank. She'll go for anything loopy. Intelligent old bird, too. Don't think I'm saying she's round the bend. She isn't. But it just seems as though certain things she can't see straight."

Coffin rang the bell again.

"I tell you it's no use."

"Wait a minute"—and Coffin listened. "I can hear footsteps." There was a dragging slithering noise from the other side of the door. He bent down and looked through the letter-box, then he drew back with an exclamation.

"What can you see?" asked the man eagerly.

"A face," said Coffin, "a great red face."

"Can't be her then; she doesn't usually look red. More the pale sort." He sounded thoughtful. "Maybe I'd better get my key."

"The door's opening."

She stood there silently, swaying unsteadily before them, with her face red and puffed and her hair blown awry.

Take it all in all, she was a surprise to Coffin.

She looked at them morosely, screwing up her eyes in the light. "What do you want?"

Her landlord from the shop whistled. "You're as drunk as an owl, my girl."

"Are you Mrs. Beaufort?" asked Coffin.

She did not answer, but swayed towards them, waving her hands and opening the door even wider.

"Course she's Mrs. Beaufort," said her landlord. "As much as she's anything. Don't believe it's her name at all, but it's what she likes. Here, hold up, Katy old girl."

"Well, I'm damned," said Coffin. "Are you sure?"

Mrs. Beaufort lifted her head, and it was an untidy one, and said: "I'm not drunk." Then she reeled a little. "I don't drink."

"She doesn't, you know," said the landlord, worried. "Someone been feeding you the stuff, old lady?" He was quite gentle and kind with her.

Coffin grunted. He had been studying her face closely. "We'd better get her in."

Between them they half-lifted and half-walked Mrs. Beaufort up her long flight of stairs. She kept up a steady murmur of conversation in Coffin's ear all the time. "I can fly," she whispered. "Did you know? I have the secret of levitation. I'm flying now."

"Are you, old girl?" Her landlord was sweating under her weight. "Well, fly a little higher, will you? You're leaning on me." He looked at Coffin. "One step forward and two back, ain't it?"

The sitting-room upstairs was a small neat room, impeccably tidy. A table stood by the window, and on it was a tea-tray with cups and saucers, milk, sugar, and a plate of biscuits. Two chairs were drawn up to the table, and a third lay on the floor as if just knocked over.

Coffin put his hand on the teapot to test the warmth; it was quite cold.

"Give us a hand," gasped his companion. "She's coming on violent."

Coffin swung round to see that Mrs. Beaufort, presumably attempting flight, was hurling herself and her companion to the ground. He rushed forward to help and together they got her to sit on the sofa which was drawn up to the hearth.

"You know, she's very strong," said Coffin; he studied her face, which was flushed and red and deceptively drowsy. "Much too strong."

"Wonder what she's been drinking? Must have dynamite in it. Wish I could lay my hands on anything as powerful." He sniffed. "Can't smell it, you know."

"I've noticed that."

"And yet she must have had a basinful."

"Not drunk," said a voice from the sofa; it was a muffled, sodden voice but there was a far-away indignation in it. And as if this was an excitement to her Mrs. Beaufort shot to her feet, leapt onto the table, and clutched the electric light.

"She'll kill herself," cried her landlord.

"Or us," said Coffin who was grimly hanging on to her ankles.

They pulled her back. But as suddenly as it had come, the energy left her, and she was limp again.

"Funniest drunk I ever saw," murmured the landlord.

Coffin looked at her but said nothing; soon it was impossible to say anything. A tremendous noise filled the room, bursting through the windows from the street outside, a great brassy clanging of bells.

"What in heaven's name is that?" Coffin looked out. A great red fire engine had come round the corner, bells ringing, and stopped outside the door. Already the firemen were running forward with ladders, and the crash of glass sounded from below. It drew a cry of anguish from the shop-owner.

"My windows!"

There was one more crash and the owner quickly dropped his share of Mrs. Beaufort into Coffin's arms and rushed downstairs shouting.

"Where's the fire," a man's deep bass voice was calling.

"My door's open. No need to break in," was the angry response; too late, however, for there was a further tinkle of glass.

A ladder rattled against the window, but before Coffin could speak to the face that appeared, his attention was distracted by something else. Mrs. Beaufort was being very sick.

A white ambulance sped silently and unnoticed up to the door and two ambulance men carried a stretcher up the stairs.

These at least Coffin welcomed. He deposited Mrs. Beaufort upon their stretcher. "You'd better get her to hospital," he said briefly to them. "And quickly, too. She's been poisoned. One of the hyoscine group, I shouldn't wonder."

Out in the street more people had arrived and were noisily assessing the situation. A black police car had drawn up at the kerb.

Eventually the surprised face of one of Coffin's Oxford police friends appeared at the top of the stairs. "What's this? A riot?" He looked down at the stretcher, "What's happened to her?"

"Poisoned I think."

"And who called out the whole circus?"

"That's right," said Coffin. "Who did?"

A voice came from the stretcher, it was weak and faint, but there was, amazingly, a hint of pride in it.

"I did," it said huskily. "Called one, called 'em all."

"Practical old duck," commented Coffin, looking down on her admiringly. "*You* weren't going to die easily were you, old lady?"

She managed to smile. "Not going to die in this town. Born in the sound of Bow Bells and going to die there." And all the spirit which had seen her, and millions like her, through two wars and two bombardments, shone for a moment before she closed them.

Coffin patted her hand. "You won't go just yet, mum," he said gently.

The local Inspector and Coffin stood aside to watch the ambulance men get the stretcher down the stairs.

"You know who she is?" asked Coffin. "But, of course you do. And if she's Mrs. Beaufort then who did I see before when I called in Chancellor Hyde Street?"

"I could make a guess," said his colleague. "I could make a guess."

"I bet you could," said Coffin, "and I'll tell you a secret: so could I."

He looked across the room to the tea-cups on the table. The classic symbol of sociability. "Have a cup of tea, dear? The kettle's just on the boil, I can have it ready in a second. I could fancy one myself."

"Two cups you see. Two women drinking together." He was speaking aloud. "Who was the other one?" Then he corrected himself. "No, not who, I know that, I think. *Where* is the other one?"

But after a moment's thought he decided he knew that, too.

They must go to Chancellor Hyde Street.

"We shall have to get her quickly now," said the local man. He looked at Coffin.

"We shall have to do more than that." Coffin had unconsciously assumed control. "She's gone off the rails. Running crazy. What we've got to do now is to stop her before she gets to the *others*." He was prepared to underline this statement: "And what's more, we can't tell exactly who she has on her list. How could we have guessed that she would try to get rid of the poor old girl here? And just because she did the charing up and down Chancellor Hyde Street."

He calculated quickly. The young man Ezra, the girl Rachel (but unknown to him he was already too late for Rachel), the doctor, because somewhere there must be a doctor, and Mrs. Springer.... God help me if she gets Ted Springer's missus, he thought. He'll have my life and I don't blame him. He ran over his conversation with Joyo on the doorstep. Surely there had been nothing that could have made her think of Mrs. Springer again? But the risk wasn't worth running. "I can think of three people we can't take any risks over, and a fourth who is only an hypothesis and who must be found as well as protected."

The local man spoke again: "If it's like you say we'd better get on the telephone. We don't know if she's going to deliver her presents in person do we? She's quite likely to have used the post."

"You think of the nastiest things," said Coffin.

"She seems quite a daisy. I wouldn't like us not to give her a big welcome. Let's organise it, shall we?"

There was great seriousness behind the joke. The situation was as tight as a drum.

So they sent out their telephone messages, warning other policemen in other districts and sending them scurrying out in all directions like ants.

Even at that moment a young detective constable in plain clothes was outside the door of the house in Chancellor Hyde Street. He had rung the bell and had no answer. Now he was listening. His instructions were that he was to cause no alarm, but to be quiet and discreet. "She's a bomb with the fuse loose," was the way his Divisional Inspector had put it, "and I don't want you handling her alone." This description was more than enough to make the young policeman, a lad from a village north of Banbury and new to Oxford, act with great caution, even though his superior had gone on to add unkindly: "I'm not worrying about what she might do to you, but what she might do to a lot of other people if the mood took her."

So after ringing the bell once more, and incidentally thus alerting the Major, he returned to the nearest telephone.

"She's there all right," he reported, "but lying doggo and doesn't answer the bell."

MRS. SPRINGER was having a quiet, happy day when the parcel came. It was a small parcel and arrived by letter-post. Stanley had just discovered her lipstick and was decorating himself and the house when it came so she put the parcel aside while she cleaned him up. Stanley had done a good job with the coral red lipstick and she took some time on the operation.

"Naughty boy," she said reprovingly. "Aunty won't have any lipstick for herself." As she rubbed at his face, she was thinking of her little present. Ted quite often sent her something; in a mysterious way, known only to his friends and himself, he managed to send her small gifts from good shops. Ted had excellent taste, as was perhaps necessary in his trade, and he never bothered with the second rate. "Dear old Ted," thought his wife. "Wonder what it is? Feels just a bit heavy for chocolates.

Might be scent. Don't think it's a bit of jewellery."
Then another problem struck her, "Now what's it
for? Why has he sent it? Have I got any anniver-
saries? Not my birthday, nor our wedding day,
anyway he sent me the lipstick for that. Bless the
boy, he's plasterd with it, too. Oh Stanley, they call
this stuff kiss-proof and it's certainly clinging to
you."

After she had finished with Stanley, she got out
a scrubbing brush and started on the wall. She had
no sooner finished with this than Stanley's mother
appeared. She was a large healthy friendly woman.

"Hello kid," she said to Stanley. "Oh look,
Nance, he knows me, you can see it in his face.
Well, I've got news."

"What?" Nancy looked alarmed.

"I'm in the pudding-club again."

"What?" said Nancy again, but this time in
horror. "And after poor little Stanley? Don't you
ever learn?"

"Not much good me learning, is it?" asked
Stanley's mother, seating herself. "If others don't."
She lit a cigarette. "September it will be."

"You haven't hurried yourself telling me."

"Wasn't sure. Oh I do hope it'll be a little girl. A
dear little girl. Stanley's daddy is just longing for a
little girl and so am I. He was ever so pleased. Another little God Bless' 'Em, he said to me."

"You never used to talk like that," reproved Nancy. "Now you always talk in slang. You get it from Stanley's father." (Both women continually referred in this oblique way to Stanley's father so that an outsider might have wondered about him, but in fact he and Stanley's mother were respectably married). "I can remember when you and I were at school and you were always top in English composition. Well, there's one thing, you'll have to stay at home and look after them both. I can't manage another beside Stanley, and Ted will be home by September."

"You'll see me over the worst, dear?"

They went on talking comfortably; Nancy was really delighted at the thought of another baby coming within her grasp, and was making a resolution that, Ted nothwithstanding, she, and not its mother, was going to be the one to bring it up.

Neither of them noticed Stanley and the dog undoing the parcel. The parcel was well tied up with string, but the dog was cleverer than Stanley and chewed it loose. Inside was a small wooden box of stuffed dates which the dog sniffed at and turned away from disappointed. Stanley liked them, though, and sat down quietly eating them.

When the door bell went no one was welcoming to the policeman who stood there. They were slow to take in what he was talking about? Threats? Danger? Poison? They didn't understand.

"No one has threatened me," said Nancy, "I know how to look after myself thank you. And if I didn't know I wouldn't ask the police. Always go to a good lawyer, my Ted told me."

"Can't trust the police," agreed her friend sagely. But Nancy did not care for this either. "That's your opinion," she said briskly, "and no doubt you've earned your right to it. I trust them but I don't want to *see* them."

The constable turned to go. "All right. I've warned you. It's up to you. Don't say I didn't tell you, that's all. And take my tip, watch out for any mysterious little bundles."

"Wait a minute." Nancy had been thinking. "I did have a parcel. I thought it was from Ted, but I don't actually know because I never opened it. Oh I expect it was," and she turned to look for it.

Then they saw Stanley; he had eaten all of the dates and was sitting there surrounded by bits of torn paper and chewed string.

His mother gave a little scream, then started to cry.

IN DR. STEINER'S waiting-room a new notice had been pinned by the door. It gave his apologies and explained that he had been taken away for an emergency operation; Dr. Browne would be taking over his patients meanwhile.

"Perforated ulcer," his receptionist was explaining briskly. "No, no, he's doing very well." But to herself she admitted that he was not doing as well as all that, and that the ulcer, which after all, was under treatment, ought not to have burst. "What the hell had he been doing with himself? He'd been worrying over something, or was it some sudden strain?"

The cleaning woman poked her head round the door. She had been tidying up and complaining bitterly at the same time about the broken window. No one could explain how it had got broken, but her theory that there had been a burglar was supported by the slight disarray of the doctor's surgery where his desk, usually so orderly, was littered with papers and stained with grubby fingermarks. They had told the police and a detective was expected every minute.

"I've got some coffee heating," she said. "Why not have a cup while you're waiting?"

They sat companionably side by side before their steaming cups of coffee. The receptionist took a sip, then she wrinkled her nose. "You just made this or has it been standing?"

"I made it as soon as I arrived. There was a packet of fresh coffee waiting on the mat and I used that. I suppose the Doctor must have ordered it before he was taken bad and no one thought to stop the errand boy bringing it round."

"I suppose so. I should empty the pot, it's too bitter." The receptionist got up and walked over to the card index. "Who's been playing about with this? You touched it, Mrs. Home?"

"No indeed." Mrs. Home was indignant. "You know I never lay hands on it. The Doctor told me never to touch it and I never do. We've been burgled, I tell you."

The nurse was rapidly flipping through the cards. "Well, some have been pulled out. I don't know if any have gone. I shall have to check." She was some time working quietly away at this checking, absorbed and intent, not thinking about Mrs. Home. Eventually she raised her head. "One *is* gone, one complete set as far as I can tell. And it's Dr. Manning's. And that is odd," she was thinking aloud, "because I believe she was his last... Mrs. Home! Mrs. Home, are you all right?"

She got up in alarm: Mrs. Home was clearly not all right; she had been drinking coffee all the morning, and it looked as though she was one of the people that the police warning was going to reach too late.

EZRA WAS AWAY at the hospital when a college messenger delivered a little packet to him.

This little packet had been placed on the messenger's table earlier that day by a hand that no one saw. It must have been a woman because men were not allowed in this college, which was a women's college, before midday, and the parcel was placed there well before that time.

All the same the parcel was late in arriving. The messenger had a slight accident with his bicycle in the morning and so he had to deliver everything on foot that day. The Oxford college messenger service is well organised and efficient, but it depends entirely on the bicycle; no self-respecting messenger would dream of borrowing a car or going on a bus. The messenger was, therefore, very slow in getting to Ezra's lodging, where he arrived late in the evening.

This was luck for Ezra because he was then out with Rachel at the hospital. But for this delay he might very soon have been lying there with her. He was specially fond of stuffed dates.

As it was he did not see them until he came in from the hospital, when he was too much preoccupied with Rachel to want to eat. He looked at them, hardly taking in the oddness of such a present. He had no more idea than the man in the moon what was happening although he had grasped that what had befallen Rachel was no accident. He had no idea even of how much time had passed since she had been taken ill. He was just surprised to see that it was daylight again.

"Better ring up Marion," he decided. He had relied on Marion so long that to do so now was automatic. He dialled the number, but for a long time there was no response. The bell continued to ring and no one answered. He was about to put the instrument down when in Marion's house the receiver was lifted. "Hello," said Ezra. He got no answer. There was the sound of breathing and that was all.

He stood there for a moment surprised and alarmed. Then he put the receiver down and decided to walk to see Marion. When he was at the door his telephone rang again.

It was a call from the hospital. He could hardly hear the words but he thought there was hope in the voice; it was Rachel's mother speaking and she was asking Ezra to come round to the hospital at once.

He hurried out, then he discovered he was still clutching the box of dates. He tossed it to his landlady's little daughter. "Present," he said and ran down the steps.

THE POLICE WERE TRYING, with varying degrees of success, to protect the people they thought might be threatened.

But the one person they could not reach was Marion.

TEN

IN THE ROOM FACING the jungle garden of Marion's house, one woman was destroying another, stripping her of everything both mental and physical that had gone to make her up.

She was tearing away her pretensions.

"You thought you were a scholar," said Joyo. "Ha, ha, we can both see the joke there, I hope. A scholar means a person who learns and you've never learnt, have you, sweety-pie? You've never learnt about me or why I hated you. So I'm telling you now: I hated you because you destroyed my life. As simple as that. And for me as complicated."

She was destroying her home: tearing books from the shelves, pictures from the walls, even cutting down in her anger the very curtains because Marion had chosen them.

She was ripping up Marion's clothes. Marion herself, bound by cords stronger than steel wire, was helpless, past even seeing what was going on perhaps. But how can we know what another person really sees? Is their yellow sun our yellow sun?

Is it the same yellow? The same sun! We cannot know. So perhaps Marion did see.

Joyo talked away.

"I'm just cutting up your clothes. Well, you won't need them any longer and I'm sure I don't want them. You had the taste in clothes of a rabbit, Marion, all greenery-yallery." Education was coming in Joyo as she talked, as well as vulgarity; who could have told till now that she had read Carlyle? Then she found a bunch of her horror comics on a chair. "Bet they made your jaw drop, sister dear. I suppose we might as well acknowledge each other as sisters now. Sisters beneath the skin."

She attacked even Marion's humanity.

"You're not even a human being, Marion. You can't be. I am, and we can't both be, can we?"

Joyo was filled with restless energy. She could not stop moving and she could not stop talking, although her speech was growing wilder and noisier, and her face getting redder.

"I'm not doing this because I love you," she said, with mordant humour. "Don't run away with the idea that this hurts me more than it hurts you. I'm loving every minute of it." She checked herself. "I mustn't talk too loud or that dear old maid of a Major next door will think you are talking to yourself. That would be rich, wouldn't it? *You* talking to yourself."

She paused for a moment in her task of destruction.

"I shall be obliged to kill you, Marion, as I expect you can see. Why did I kill my husband? (Yes, he *was* my husband, poor little shrimp, and quite uxorious, too.) Why shall I kill you? It's very simple: to save myself. He would have destroyed me in the end, and so would you. I recognise your power, Marion, even though I despise you." She staggered a little. "I'm just a little drunk. I've had some of that brew I gave the other two. Not so much, of course. I want *them* to die, they know about me you see, but I only wanted just enough to excite *me*. I often use it. Medieval witches used it. And also some of those queer tribes you and the girl Rachel are keen on. Henbane. And the irony is, Marion, that you taught me the uses of Henbane, and you grew it in your garden. You ought to have been keener on gardening, dear.... I think I will just sit down for a moment." She sat down, but still went on talking. "So you will die and be dead. Dead but not buried. For I am afraid that, practically speaking, it will be impossible for me to bury you. So you will have to mortify standing up, Marion.... You'll do that good. I always thought you were half dead anyway."

Joyo stood up and got down the huge mirror from the wall; it was all she could do to carry it.

"Down on your knees, Marion, kneel down and pray. There you are, naked and ashamed. Not that you are much of a prayer, I really think that's what I hate most about you, your damned self-sufficiency. Is the intellect really enough for you now, Marion? You never thought that in the end sheer physical strength would get on top, did you?

"They say that all is in the mind, but is it I wonder?"

In spite of herself Joyo's voice was altering, growing weaker, higher, and yet more gentle. She began to feel her throat tightening as she looked in the mirror.

Presently there were tears.

"It's me that's crying, not *you,* Marion," she said sadly. "And of all things—I'm crying for you."

And after that there was no more noise except the banging on the wall from the Major next door, who was getting anxious.

ELEVEN

BY THE TIME EZRA got to the house in Chancellor Hyde Street it was mid-morning of the next day, Wednesday. Rachel was better, he had seen her and talked to her. It was because of what she had murmured to him that he was on his way round now. He should have been earlier, that was what he kept muttering to himself, rather like the White Rabbit, but after leaving Rachel in the small hours of the morning and sending a telegram to her parents who characteristically had already flooded him with long and expensive telegrams of bewildering complexity, he had fallen asleep in his chair.

There was a policeman standing outside the house, and as he stood staring, two more men came down the little path to the gate. It seemed incongruous that the cat Sammy should still be sitting there sunning himself on the gate-post. When Ezra saw the policemen he felt a sense of doom, as if he drunk the poison that Rachel and Mrs. Beaufort had shared. In a sense, he considered, so he had; you can take poison in different ways; through the mouth, like the two women, through the ear, like Hamlet's father, and through the mind, as he had.

All the same, he had not fully taken in all that Rachel in her confused and incoherent way had told him, as he was soon to discover. They knew by now that Rachel had been poisoned in Marion's house, but Rachel seemed to show more fear *for* Marion than of her.

But when he saw the policemen he knew that whatever had happened he had been too late.

"You can't go in," said Coffin. "Indeed there's no point." And he added sadly, "We've got our murderer, poor soul."

Ezra was wrenched between a desire to know and a fear of what he must learn. "Dr. Manning?" he said hesitantly. "Is she all right?"

"I'm afraid she's dead," said Coffin simply, before his colleague, who clearly had something to say, could speak. "I hope, indeed I think, she was dead before the Major called us round. We were coming anyway."

The Major's narrative was simple. He had been sitting quietly in his kitchen at work on his table silver when the noise started. He pointed out that it was because he was so quiet that he had heard the noise which was not then over-loud. He usually had the gramophone on when he polished the silver, as it gave him something to think about. But that evening he already had plenty to think about: he had been puzzled by the bonfire which both he and Coffin had observed. As far as he knew this was the first time his neighbour had shown any interest in the garden, let alone to burn up the weeds of which he would be the first to admit there were far too many. He had studied the bonfire and noticed that it was composed of a weed of one sort only, and not a very pretty weed either, nor one that he was readily able to identify. A little work with his *Dictionary of British Herbs and Plants* very soon enabled him to make a guess, though. One picture in the book had been particularly clear and helpful. Henbane as a poison is hardly any trouble to prepare. You can boil it up, if you like, or just sprinkle the seeds in any bit of cooking you happen to be doing, a pot of coffee, say, or a cup of tea. A couple of hundred seeds can kill a man, and the plant is prolific, so this quantity is no problem.

Joyo had then burnt the weeds. But what she and the Major did not know was that the act of burning releases a powerful and intoxicating poison. The very smoke is deadly.

The Major had put a hand unsteadily to his suddenly hot forehead. It was about henbane he was thinking when the noises began. Just at first he had thought, in his housewifely way, that someone next door was raking out the kitchen boiler. But he speedily recalled, as he had every reason to know from the mammoth piles of rubbish that appeared on dust-bin day, that next door had no kitchen boiler and heated their water by gas. Then the

noises had altered their character and revealed
themselves as more of a banging and a dragging
than a scraping. This was a change which did not
cheer him up at all. The Major was now thoroughly alarmed. He was sure he could hear furni-
ture being moved and pictures being dragged
roughly from walls. A vivid picture began to form
before his eyes and one which he was to learn later
was not far off the truth.... "Looting and ravag-
ing," he thought reminiscently. "Parhadubad,
1947, that's where I last heard noises like that." He
went on listening. For some reason his unconscious mind tossed up to him the ridiculous nursery rhyme of Humpty-Dumpty.

>"Humpty-Dumpty had a great fall,
>And all the king's horses and all the king's
>men,
>Couldn't put Humpty together again."

Once Humpty was shattered nothing and no one
could put Humpty together again into one whole.

Then the voice began. It started in low tones that
he had difficulty in hearing, but soon it was
shrieking. He walked up the stairs and went into his
sitting-room where he pressed his ear to the wall; he
couldn't hear clearly or continuously, but he could
hear in snatches. He could hear Dr. Manning's
name. "Marion, Marion," the voice was shouting.

He had no difficulty in identifying the voice as that of the strange painted woman he had sometimes seen around Dr. Manning's house and at once summed up as no lady. Certainly no lady would carry on as she was doing now. She sounded drunk. He had some reason to believe she did drink because the grocer in Walton Street had hinted it, adding with a rum look that she had called herself Dr. Manning's cousin. That was a lie to start with, because Dr. Manning had flatly denied having one. They *looked* more like sisters.

Then the voice had changed again, this time the Major had a terrifying thought of two women fighting; one of them shrieking with anger, and the other one, silent and terrified, fighting for her life.

When all fell silent he became really frightened and telephoned the police.

"I think there are two dead women next door," he cried in alarm. He was not far from the truth.

Coffin told all this to Ezra, adding that the police had been at work all night. He himself looked exhausted. As he was speaking, Ezra noticed activity at the door. Then he took in the significance of the long anonymous-looking van. They were taking Marion away.

"I want to see Dr. Manning," he said firmly. "I'm one of her oldest friends. I want to see her."

Perhaps he cherished some hope that there had been a mistake and that Marion, dear, kind, loving

Marion, was not dead. Silently they led him into the house. It was in disorder enough, but Joyo, in the time allowed her, had not achieved all the destruction she had planned.

"How did Marion die?" asked Ezra as they walked through the tiny hall. He had been nerving himself to ask this question for some time.

Coffin hesitated. Then he said: "We think it was a heart attack. Her heart had probably been weakened by her bomb experiences in the war, and then, of course, she was drugged...."

It was a relief to Ezra that she had not been brutally murdered, and he said so.

Coffin just shook his head. He looked at the young man, not after all so much his junior, but years younger in experience of life, and said to himself: "You've got a lot to learn, young chap."

At the door to the sitting-room Coffin stood aside and let Ezra look in. There was a long silence. Then Ezra turned to Coffin.

"But there's only one woman there."

"Yes," said Coffin. "Only one woman there. Dr. Manning and her other self are united in the end." He lifted up her left hand and fitted on it the wedding ring he had got from Mrs. Springer. "There it goes," he said, "back where it came from, the ring from Dr. Manning's first wedding."

Joyo and Marion were dead, as they had lived, in the same body.

"I'VE SETTLED IN MY MIND to go to London," said Ezra, who was talking to Rachel. She was leaning back against her pillows, recovered and, therefore, inclined to be ashamed of the private room and nurse, luxuries which her parents anxious, and extravagant as always, had showered on her upon their return. "I must get better soon," worried Rachel. "What must all this be costing? Hope they can pay the bill," she added doubtfully. But she had heard what Ezra said and laid her hand on his.

"I'd see Marion everywhere. I couldn't bear to stay. Besides, you were right all the time. I shall be better away. More resolute." And he squared his shoulders hopefully.

Rachel nodded; she looked quite herself again, although thinner and paler. All the victims of the poison, now known as a preparation of henbane, were getting on well. Of all of them, only Stanley in London had taken a really dangerous amount of the stuff, and even he was all right. He had solved it in his own way. "Sicked it all up," said Mrs. Springer through her tears, "the dear clever little fellow." This was the only time in his life that Stanley had yet earned the epithet. "It just shows doesn't it, that nature gives a special protection to people like him. He just sicked it up like a little dog." Good came out of this episode for Stanley: the doctor who saw him realised at once that his dullness was not a cross to be borne for the rest of his life but a simple case of thyroid deficiency and that Stanley, once treated, would be, if not clever, at any rate as normal as his parents.

"I have two careers open to me, as far as I can see," said Ezra, with grim amusement. "I can become a successful novelist. Or I can become a distinguished theatre critic. You choose."

"I shall leave it to you," said Rachel. "I have complete faith in your judgement."

"Well, I'm glad you admit at last that I've got a mind," said Ezra, much gratified; now he and Rachel might get somewhere.

Rachel smiled and pressed his hand. The truth was that she loved him for quite other reasons, for the way he held his head, and the way he crossed a road, and even for his streaks of silliness.

"Very true, my love," she said, practising.

"Don't overdo it, Rachel," murmured Ezra suspiciously. But they sat happily hand in hand for a few minutes. Ezra who had once been close enough to Marion to be thought to be her son (and not only by Joyo either) had now drawn away. He was changing, moving, growing closer to Rachel. It was inevitable and natural and Marion, had she been there to see, would have observed it with wry amusement.

"It seems awful to let happiness come out of unhappiness," said Rachel suddenly.

Ezra nodded. "It's even more awful to know that you've been completely in the dark about one aspect of someone very close to you. I thought of Marion as the soul of normality. Almost stolid, except that one knew that someone who had done the work she had could never be called that. And all the time she was two people. She had two selves, like the famous Miss Sally Beauchamp; Sally had three selves, I think, all completely different and distinct, and only one of them knowing about the other two. That's awful, too, if you like to think about it; Marion herself had no idea about the other one, although Joyo knew all about *her*."

Rachel nodded. "I knew, too, by the end. I did see Joyo once or twice you know, and on that last day before I was ill I guessed. I saw her face to face; usually she was clever about people she knew, and avoided them. That's why she tried to kill me."

"The doctors think it started on that expedition: that the shock caused by the death of her husband split Marion in two and a second personality peeled off."

"And not a nice one either," said Rachel with a shudder. "That poor little second husband. Killed just because he put in his claim to her life."

"The second marriage dates from another bad patch: the bomb injury threw Marion right back. In between, the wound in her personality, if one can call it that, must have healed, although everyone who knew her agrees that she was never quite the same after the Central American trip," Ezra sighed.

"But Ezra, can one aspect of a person kill if the other part isn't equally willing? Wouldn't it be somehow like the response to hypnotism, that one wouldn't, couldn't do anything totally alien to the mind?"

"I don't know. Probably. But remember, *we* never saw the real Marion, the whole person. She died when her first husband was killed. We saw only one restricted character." He added thoughtfully: "I don't believe she was ever as good as we thought she was. We largely invented the character of Marion: we saw that she was spontaneous, amusing, clever, affectionate, and deduced from all this that she was good, too. Good to *us,* was all we really meant. But we had plenty of pointers the other way if we had seen them. The Professor warned us, he almost warned me against Marion once, and the Major knew, too, he was always very reserved about Marion. And there must be a doctor. I know she consulted a doctor, although heaven knows he seems to have done her no good."

(Poor Dr. Steiner had no luck, even his proposal to cure Marion by sending her to a special nursing home of which he had discovered the address got him no credit, no reward, and lost him his client.)

"What about her first husband?" asked Rachel suddenly. "He died, too, you know. Had she something to do with that, do you suppose?"

Then Ezra sat silent for a long time. "How can we know?" he asked. "How can we ever know?"

SO OF ALL THE PEOPLE who had known and loved Marion only the Major who had overheard something of her last spoken words knew that Joyo had died, not in anger and hate, but because she knew in the end that she had loved what she had destroyed.

DESERT SINNER
RALPH McINERNY

First Time in Paperback

A Father Dowling Mystery

TRUE CONFESSIONS
The Wilson case was delightful fare for the gossip-addicted—a Vegas showgirl lucks out and marries an impossibly rich aging playboy, takes out a large insurance policy...then kills him.

Lots of people are intrigued by Stacey Wilson, her crime and her confession, including Father Roger Dowling. And why is that handsome young man calculatedly wooing police captain Phil Keegan's love-struck secretary? Is it as innocent as it seems?

Father Dowling believes that Stacey Wilson was wrongfully convicted. And that what lies beneath the surface of an open-and-shut case will prove deadly....

"McInerny builds superb psychological portraits...."
—*Chicago Sun Times*

Available in December at your favorite retail stores.

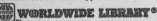

Take 3 books and a surprise gift FREE

SPECIAL LIMITED-TIME OFFER

Mail to: **The Mystery Library™**
3010 Walden Ave.
P.O. Box 1867
Buffalo, N.Y. 14269-1867

YES! Please send me 3 free books from the Mystery Library™ and my free surprise gift. Then send me 3 mystery books, first time in paperback, every month. Bill me only $3.69 per book plus 25¢ delivery and applicable sales tax, if any*. There is no minimum number of books I must purchase. I can always return a shipment at your expense and cancel my subscription. Even if I never buy another book from the Mystery Library™, the 3 free books and surprise gift are mine to keep forever. 415 BPY ANQ2

Name	(PLEASE PRINT)	
Address		Apt. No.
City	State	Zip

* Terms and prices subject to change without notice. N.Y. residents add applicable sales tax. This offer is limited to one order per household and not valid to present subscribers.

© 1990 Wolrdwide Library.

MYS-94

LONG DAY MONDAY

PETER TURNBULL

First Time in Paperback

A Glasgow P Division Mystery

IT BEGAN WITH A MISSING CHILD

A boy of ten. Then a stolen car. And finally, the body of a young woman found in a shallow grave beside a road in Lanarkshire. And at this scene of morbidity and murder was a fluffy toy rabbit.

Call it intuition of an old jaded cop, but suddenly Ray Sussock of the P Division in Glasgow knew there was another body nearby...that had been there for twenty-five years. To the horror of the investigators, the fields of Lanarkshire begin to give up their dead. Forensic evidence indicates the victims had all endured periods of captivity before their death.

And now, beneath the harsh glare of a naked bulb, a terrified boy waits for this final embrace with a killer.

"An outstanding series."   —*Publishers Weekly*

Available in January at your favorite retail stores.

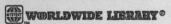